AN ENDLESS QUEST FOR SPIRITUAL TRUTH

A PRACTICAL GUIDE TO EVERYDAY SPIRITUALITY

D1561448

Eric Chifunda

Fulton Books, Inc.
Meadville, PA

First originally published by Fulton Books 2017

ISBN 978-1-63338-322-7 (Paperback)
ISBN 978-1-63338-323-4 (Digital)

Printed in the United States of America

CONTENTS

What Is Life? • Answers to Life • Life Goes On • Are
We Doing Enough? • Soul Has Answers • Thank
You, Stranger • On the Journey • Giving Up Life of
Attachment • Anger • Factors That Lead to a More
Fulfilling Life • The Purpose of Our Existence • Looking
Good From Within • Cycles of Life • Turning on a New
Leaf • A Sense of Clarity • Changing to Who We Are
Truly • Staying Connected With The Essence Of God •
Getting the Truth from Divine Spirit • Listening More
to the Voice of Divine Spirit • Loving Life • How Can
One Love God Daily? • The Power of Love • Non-
attached Love • God's Answer For You • Fulfilling
One's Work • Love, the Key • Acts of Love • Change •
Elements of Love • Love Is the Key to All Life • Loving
Self As Soul, Not As Ego Self • Love Conquers Time
• Love: The Key to Success • Brotherly Love • God Is
the Essence of All Life • Facing Life • What You Give
to Life, You Get Back in Return • The Key to Life •
Dreaming Your Way to Success • Letting Go the Lower
Self • Loving the Other as Soul • Organizing Your Life
• Time Heals • Meeting Change • Going Back to the

Way Things Used to Be • Attitude • Reaching a Goal • Doing Everything You Have Agreed to Do • Finishing Things Pending • Loss Is Gain • Spiritual Resolution to a Business Impasse • A Prayer of Thanks • The Act of Love • The Past Resurfaces • Pains of Awareness • The Paradox of the Voice of *God*

You Are an Aspect of God • When Love Comes, Life Begins Its Ascent • Becoming a Conscious God Child • When You Love Unconditionally, Love Comes Back to You A Hundredfold • Opening Your Heart to More Love • Divine Spirit, My True Friend • Your Relationship with God • The Daily Presence of God • Simply Be • Help from God • Unlocking God's Treasures • You Are Soul • Living a Life of Divine Spirit • Passing the Gift • Allowing in Divine Spirit's Influence • Listening to the Inner Voice of *God* • Engaging in Activities that Will Expand Your Life beyond Where You Are • Listening to Divine Spirit and Following It without Question • Loving for the Good of All • Living a Life Filled with Love • A Life of Love Guided by the Will of God • Obedience to God • Loving God in the Moment • God Needs You • The Invisible Hand of God • Your Daily Guide • God's Actions through You

Love and Truth • Love Becomes You as You Become Love • Climbing to Greater Spiritual Heights • Serving Life • Living Life Fully • Blessings from Divine Spirit • Living a Detached Life • What Is Surrender? • Love from Unexpected Places • Different Manifestations of Love • Talk Love Today • Love: The Key to All Life • Giving Back to Life • You Can Have Your Life in Order Again • Getting Out of Trouble • Serving Life

with Love• Appreciating God More • Sharing Love •
How Can I Serve God More? • Everything Changes
with Love • When True Love Enters One's Life • A Life
of Action • Love Is a Journey • How Do You Live in
Accord with God's Will? • Moving On • Messengers
of Love • Loving Others • Love's Way • Doing Things
in God's Name • The Key To Spirituality • Working
with God on a Daily Basis • Becoming a More Realized
Spark of God • Living Life to Its Fullest • Learning How
to Survive • Help from Divine Spirit • Giving Love to
Others • Love and Relationships • Be the Best that You
Can Ever Be • Pure Love

Journey Back Home • God Speaks to Us in Many
Ways • Following the Voice of *God* • The Key to
Noninterference • Going Beyond • Helping Others •
Letting Go So God Can Take Over • Moving Closer
to God • Loyal Servant • The Paradox of Loving God
• How to Love God • Listening to the Voice of God
• Key to Living a Full Life • God in Charge • Serving
God • Greater Love for God • Expression of Soul •
What You Are in Truth and in Spirit • Making Life
Better • In God's Hands • Putting Love Into Things
We Do • Getting Higher To The Next Level • God, the
Center of Your Life • God Is in You as You Are in God •
Spiritual State

The Heart Center • Accepting Gifts from Divine Spirit
• Truth and Love Yield Greater Love • Gifts from *God*?
• Steps to Receiving Gifts from *God* • Creating Hallow
Grounds Upon Which We Walk • Loving Wisely •
Establishing A Better Relationship With Life And God
• Spiritual Masters Among Us • Loving God Knowing

PREFACE

Growing up, I wondered about life. I was in search of something beyond the usual humdrum life we seem to go through, but I couldn't put my finger on what it was. I thought I had a sense of what it was, yet not quite. It seemed real and palpable yet intangible and elusive.

It seemed far yet as near as my heartbeat. I knew with curious certainty that it was something that could show me the way. The way to a new and brighter tomorrow with a promise of freedom from the shackles of this world. I felt that I wasn't going to rest till I found it. I hoped that finding it would help unravel the mystery of my unfulfilled life.

I had a deeper, unquenchable desire to understand life in general and my life at a deeper level. Questions about who I was, where I was coming from, where I was going to and why I was here taunted me.

I often felt I was at the mercy of life—a life that seemed random. The paradox was that I felt I was alive, yet at the same time I was asleep—spiritually. Deep down within me was a yearning to wake up—spiritually. Hoping that by waking up from my apparent spiritual slumber I would begin to live a life with meaning and purpose. Not forgetting to be cognizant of the fact that life has unending traps that come in different subtle but enticing and well-packaged guises designed to lead one astray. Not forgetting how temptations constantly dog us, trying to trip us so we can yield to them. Should I yield to temptations, get trapped and fall, as I often have, I would fail in my quest for deeper truth about life. But if I had an awakened consciousness, I could muster up enough strength and courage to rise and continue on my life journey, stronger, wiser, and with clearer sight. With clearer sight, I could sidestep life's unnecessary traps that serve to cause unnecessary pain and suffering. With clearer sight, I could select to endure the pains only which are necessary for my growth.

Questions upon questions, my search for the unknown seemed unending. Finally, at the height of my long apparent futile search, feeling worn, tired, frustrated, driven to the brink of giving up the quest for the call of unknown truth, an epiphany hit me. It felt like a sharp ray of light pierced through my hardened and closed consciousness, lighting up my inner world. I caught a glimpse of a new world, at the same time I experienced a much-needed reprieve from the pressures of my daily grind, if only for a fleeting moment. Momentarily, I enjoyed a brief foretaste of heavenly joy, beyond words, that would await me should I fully awaken to this higher unknown inner reality. Suddenly, it became apparent that it's Light I have been searching for. Light emanating from a higher source I understood to be God. The Light of God to guide me along my apparent random and uncertain journey of my life. In the Light, I can awaken to higher truth, love, freedom, wisdom, and joy. In the Light, I can begin to move, live, and experience life in its fullness. Is there more to life than Light? Is Light an aspect of love, I began to wonder. A deep desire to understand love, its nature, its role, its reality, its source, and all things God began to gnaw at me. I felt that Light will lead me to higher truth. And in Light, my ardent quest for spiritual truth about life, love, and God began.

ACKNOWLEDGMENTS

I would like to express my deepest gratitude to my friend and former co-worker, Edwil Barquin, for having asked me a seemingly simple question, out of the blue, while at work. "When are you going to write your book?" he casually asked me, catching me off guard as I had not thought of writing a book at that time, though I had been privately writing in my journal my perceptions and insights about life for years without any plan to write a book. His question triggered an idea I had not thought of until that moment.

I can't fully express my sincere gratitude to Dr. Charles Malata, MD, FRSCS, MRCS for introducing me to the path of Spiritual Freedom

I also want to express my eternal gratitude to Sri Harold Klemp, my teacher, my friend, my mentor, whose teaching has inspired me beyond words.

I owe Michele Bluestone a debt of gratitude for her helpful suggestion about the book format in the early stage of the manuscript.

I would be remiss not to express my grateful thanks to my good friend, Isabel Chuang, for her unflagging support and encouragement.

A special word of thanks also belongs to Bobbi Hicks for her helpful, expert guidance and suggestions that were given so generously while I was revising this book. Additionally, my heartfelt thanks again to Bobbi for inviting me to one of her great seminars which underscored the importance of setting goals with time-lines which helped me in my timely completion of the manuscript.

My heartfelt thanks also goes to Linda Anderson, whom through a chance encounter at a seminar answered some questions I had about book publishing which helped set me on the right course.

LIFE

WHAT IS LIFE?

Life is what you make it, is a common refrain. True but not so simplistic. The truth of the matter is that there are two aspects to life: the visible outer day to day life and secondly the nonphysical, hidden, limitless, spiritual side, where night dreams appear and beyond, the one we know less about to which we pay barest attention. To understand the depth and truth about life, we need to plumb its depth.

Life is sacred as it is sustained by the life force, Divine Spirit, the essence of God. Life is designed to lead Soul back to God whence it came from. Life should progressively lead one to greater awareness and greater love for God. In the beginning, Soul, was undeveloped, untested, therefore immature. The process of growth through a variety of life experiences gradually raises Soul to a level of maturity in its conscious knowingness of its mission and relationship with God.

In the initial stage, life may seem unconnected to learning about love for God, but that of living it at a basic human level centered on one's basic physical level. The awakening of consciousness leads one to gradually, through life experiences, expand one's awareness to the point of living a life of serving others instead of self only.

Despite all the pains and joys in our life journey, as one expands in consciousness and understanding, one begins to realize that life is intended to lead one to God via love. And the difficulties we face along the way are designed to temper Soul, awaken us to our true spiritual nature—a side of us that is indestructible. This realization of our eternal nature changes the way we view life; therefore, how we live our lives.

With awakened consciousness, we are able to see that life, and our physical surroundings are not static. Though they may appear fixed, they are fluid and can be molded to our choosing to make our lives better. Despite all the pains in life, we begin to view life as not something to run away from, but to be fully lived and embraced. Such is life, such is its simplicity yet complex, and to understand it and enjoy it greatly, one must learn to recognize its profound hidden meaning which can be facilitated by awakening one's consciousness.

ANSWERS TO LIFE

There is a spiritual answer to every question. However, life does not come with a manual to guide us toward all the answers we need. During periods of turmoil, doubt, anxiety, adversity, trials, or when at crossroads, we wish God could give us easy clear answers about what to do or the right direction to go. Why doesn't God give us easy clear messages? Could it be that the messages are clear except our hearing and sight are faulty? Could it be that divine spirit is always trying to guide us in the right direction but we are either not aware, or we refuse to follow? Could it be that we hold on to old ways tenaciously that we resist new and right ways that may come about? Could it be that we have not purified our hearts enough to hear the guiding voice of God? Could it be that *God* is always present with us, but we are not always available to God through our own ignorance, pride, or stubbornness? As the Christian bible aptly states something to the effect that we have eyes, but we don't see, and we have ears, but we don't hear. This implies that our dependency on our limited physical eyes and ears do not allow us to see spiritual realities because they are outside the range of our physical senses. Hence, to view spiritual truth we have to forego the use of our limited physical senses and use our spiritual faculties that are designed to gain knowledge of spiritual truth.

It seems that our need for *God* grows greater when we are having a difficult time. Our need for help seems to make us want *God* more. Therefore we tend to be closer to God during these difficult times. And when our needs are fulfilled by the grace of God, we are the last to remember to thank *God*. At that time, our attention is no longer on God because the need for God is no longer there. Without consistent interaction with God, our understanding of God's ways will be wanting. Therefore when God speaks, we won't hear because we are not familiar with Its ways, Its language, Its voice. It seems life's answers are for those who have learned to hear and see through their spiritual eyes and ears.

To get answers, one ought to be ready to see and hear when they come. The difficulty is that life's answers may come in ways that are unexpected. Thus they may come in a way we might not recognize if our hearts are not ready and open to God's ways. Thus it takes an awakened heart to recognize, receive, and accept answers from God. If we expect to get anything of worth from life, we must do our part—that's putting in work truthfully. The more we expect from life, the harder we have to work in whatever we choose. That's the way life works. As we get a good return from life, we must be grateful. Being grateful prepares our hearts to receiving more of life's gifts. Answers come more easily to one with a grateful heart. Because a grateful heart is an open heart. And an open heart is a receptive heart. A receptive heart is a golden heart. A heart of gold is a loving heart; a loving heart has a direct link to God.

And therein lies the key to getting answers from God.

LIFE GOES ON

Life is a mystery, yet not so to those whose spiritual eyes and ears are trained and open. Life never stops here when one dies. Life stops here only as an illusion. Death never takes away life in the real spiritual sense. Life goes on, on and on beyond the reaches of human consciousness, to the very heart of God. Beyond death, beyond dreams, beyond the world of appearances as we know it here in the physical world, there's continuity of life.

There's eternal life. Life beyond our reach yet within our reach—higher life than our minds can fathom. In higher life, we find higher truth. Most people don't want truth. Yet it is in the truth that we discover a new life concept. But we need a paradigm shift to open us to a new world. A world filled with light, love, beauty unmatched here on earth. A higher world imbued with the pure light of *God* in which we can find wisdom, truth, and freedom. Therefore it is to our spiritual advantage to access this inner world beyond the portals of death that can be traversed in the now. For in the now lies the secret of the eternity of life here and beyond. We don't have to wait for death to supervene to gain a glimpse of the wondrous hidden heaven worlds. They are here and now.

ARE WE DOING ENOUGH?

God is always good for us. Good in the sense that *It* provides us all that is needed in the moment if only we can wake up to what's going on around us and through us.

But, we have to help ourselves first before It can help us. We can't sit around whole day, whole life, waiting for Divine Spirit to lower itself down to our level. Doing so, will be working against its true nature and purpose, which is always moving forward, always uplifting those who seek it in truth and sincerity.

The expression, "God helps those who help themselves" is apt here. Our role in initiating action is vital, for it determines how we receive from God. We need to do enough to open ourselves in order to receive God's gifts. In other words we have to earn the gifts. And we don't earn them by not putting effort and time in. We don't earn them by not working for them. The bigger the gift we expect, the harder we have to work.

With this attitude, life will reward us a hundred-fold. Our relationship with life will continually be harmonious and enriching. Our journey home to God will get easier as we sharpen our survival skills.

Through an improved relationship with God, our level of consciousness expands. With this expansion comes greater understanding and enjoyment of life like never imagined before. Giving us deeper meaning and purpose for our life as we become aware of our true mission. Divine spirit has the ability to open us to new ways of how God operates. It has the power to heal us emotionally, mentally, physically, and spiritually if we merit it.

It has the power to protect us in times of danger. But, are we doing enough to allow Divine Spirit in our lives to operate more freely, more willingly, at a more conscious level?

SOUL HAS ANSWERS

When you have a question about a situation you want to find out about, check with the inner, the innermost part of ourselves called Soul. Soul, an instrument of God, is equipped with foresight and insight. It has spiritual eyes that have unique ability to see through life's intricacies. Eyes that can view a situation in its totality, seeing in full view the underlying cause and effect. Effects that manifest as our daily problems we are unable to see and grasp with our limited mind and sight.

The outer that we so much depend on for answers provides little or none in the true spiritual sense. Real answers come from the inner, where possibilities are illimitable. To access answers from the inner, one needs to place attention on the inner, Divine Spirit. With this, we can get an awareness of what needs to be done. On the inner, we open up to the inner sight and voice. With our spiritual ears now open, we can hear the voice of God. We are now better positioned to tune into God's impeccable guidance. Its guidance is infallible. Equipped with the knowledge of what to do, we can now move forward, aligning our actions appropriately to meet today's life challenges. This way we can effectively fulfill our needs and be of help to other people as life unfolds. Sometimes this may require sacrifice on our part in order to render help to another. Love so rendered can have an uplifting effect on the recipient and the benefactor.

Bear in mind that any act done with sacrifice to help another in need is never in vain. It takes more for one to rise above one's comfort level in order to meet a greater need where warranted, and to that end, one shall be lifted, leaving one a changed person. Because that is the nature of love from *God* via Soul as its willing distributor to respond to the needs of the moment, and acting upon them no matter how difficult they might be.

If you want answers to life, simply look to Soul, the highest and innermost part of each one of us. Because in Soul, we can connect with God, and in that state of connectivity, we can receive answers more clearly. The challenge is how to raise one's consciousness so as to grow in awareness of oneself as Soul.

There are a few paths that purport to get one to the state of realizing oneself as Soul. Each person will determine for themselves what fits their spiritual quest till they ultimately find that which can lead them to the realization of oneself as Soul, not just by belief or speculation but in an experiential way.

THANK YOU, STRANGER

People come into our lives for a reason. Often, we don't realize why someone gets a job at our workplace. Like a gentleman who started working at my workplace. He seemed humble and unassuming in his disposition. His humble and cool demeanor belied his depth. His grace and respect for others made him appear gentle, almost soft. Yet in his own humility and self-effacing manner-isms, he commanded such immense respect. Yet, on the other hand, he was as stern as anyone could be. He was very knowledgeable in his profession. He was highly skilled yet he did not brag about it. He was humble, lov-ing, and compassionate. He treated all with respect.

I respected him for who and what he was. He was a model therapist who epitomized professionalism of high standards. He genuinely cared about my welfare and extended the same to those around him. What a Godsend! It seems he came there as an unknowing chan-nel for Divine Spirit to teach me something I needed to learn about professionalism in the early years of my career.

Sometimes Divine Spirit may use someone such as a coworker, a friend, a family member, a stranger, your boss at work, to teach us something we need in our life, often in an area of our weakness on which we need work-ing. So look around you, maybe your co-workers, what are people around you teaching you about yourself?

For that, I eternally thank you, Stranger, wherever you are, whatever noble work you are doing, for, from you, I learned valuable life lessons about professionalism.

ON THE JOURNEY

Many times on my journey to learn how to follow GOD'S guidance, I have stopped and wondered about whether I was doing the right thing or making wrong choices that would take me in the opposite, negative direction. Was I reading the signposts correctly? Was I applying the spiritual principles correctly? Was I effectively maintaining my spiritual awareness through spiritual exercises? Was I being adequately detached from situations I had become attached to? Was I maintaining proper and enough objectivity? Was I doing this and that...Questions upon questions, going on forever.

At times I made choices based on inner guidance, which sometimes came through dreams. How good my understanding of the guidance was dependent on how well I interpreted the dream. Often I was wrong because I tended to apply the principles from a logical standpoint. The dream world is a different world, whose images and experiences are open to a variety of interpretations and don't easily conform to logic. In the physical, fire is fire; in the dream world, it could mean different things to different people. The journey into the mystery of life is endless and can be complex, therefore takes great care to correctly fathom it at different levels, both deep and superficial.

GIVING UP LIFE OF ATTACHMENT

When we give up something from within and it does not come back to us, chances are that we didn't need it. So, no regrets, no loss; if anything we have gained for that may have been an obstacle to our spiritual progress.

Learning detachment makes it easier to learn how to live with *God*, in God, for *God*, and by *God*'s laws. On face value, it seems contradictory; but when we plumb the depths of it, we realize what it truly is in spiritual sense. Spirituality forms an integral part of our lives irrespective of one's religion to the extent that we all have a spiritual side. To understand it, to know it, and to live it is to live in a state of mental poverty of material desires and mental possessions. These mental possessions exist and persist because we have allowed them through our own notion of security, false sense of need for them for our survival. Yet true spiritual survival does not depend on anything in the outer world. Things of the outer world hold us in bondange through undue attachment. Unfortunately, we tend to define ourselves by identification with our material possessions. This creates fear because our dependency is on things of impermanent value. This fear influences how we conduct ourselves and how we relate to others. As a result our behaviors become shaped and dictated by our fears. This results in diminution of our latent divine character. Our lives become limited contrary Divine Spirit's nature for us. Thus it behooves us to eradicate all self-imposed limitations in our life, eliminating inner bonds to this outer world of materiality. It is by giving up life of attachment from within that we awaken to an abundant spiritual life that encompasses all aspects of our lives and brings about true fulfillment beyond measure.

ANGER

Anger is a destructive force and it is one of the passions of the mind or our human emotion. Whereas it is normal to be upset when something unpleasant happens to us, being angry is an extreme form of being upset. Without proper control of it and not understanding its destructive nature, we often allow it to spiral out of control. Additional to that, we justify it when all is said and done. Sometimes we regret it and other times we feel good about it if it affords us a false sense of pride stemming from having intimidated, beaten up, or forcibly encroached upon someone else's space, and we call it justifiable anger so as to justify our actions. In our own self-righteous way, it is always the other person's fault, we conveniently believe. We feel we have the right to be angry because we have been provoked without realizing the deleterious consequences of such emotional indulgence. We make no attempt to control it or if we try we often fail at it especially if anger is a dominant and intractable force in our life. In the fit of anger, we are liable to say things that are destructive and irrational that we would not say if we had kept our emotions in check.

It is important to recognize that words, deeds, thoughts fueled and executed with anger are always destructive. The problem is that as these actions born out of anger begin to come back as negative effect, we don't recognize their origin thus we are often unable to link them to our past actions. Unfortunately, we begin to point fingers at others, blaming everybody but ourselves. Blinded by our emotions and unable to see the causal link, we repeat the same cycle, making the same mistakes over and over and continue to suffer the effects emanating from such negative thoughts and deeds. Sooner or later it begins to have ruinous impact on our life. It is in our best interest to learn to control anger by gaining control of our mind. That is the starting point. First step is to learn to recognize its injurious effect on yourself and to whom it is directed and find techniques to minimize or bring it under control. To help bring anger under control, one can try a simple natural technique by either mentally or vocally singing an ancient natural charged sound called HU (sang as HUE) when you get angry or catch yourself getting angry.

Essentially what we are learning is how to put Soul in charge of the mind other than the other way round. As the expression aptly goes: The mind makes a bad master but a good servant.

FACTORS THAT LEAD TO A MORE FULFILLING LIFE

A fulfilling life as we know it in human state is one in which there's love, good health, material self-sufficiency, and spiritual well-being. A combination of these in a balanced manner makes for a fulfilling life. Factors that lead to such a life are many and varied. To name some of them: self-discipline, hard work, patience, clear goal setting, motivation to aspire to excellence, pursuit of a career in which you have a special ability, interest, talent, or love.

With self-discipline comes actions directed toward fulfillment of work set out to be accomplished without being distracted by other extraneous and competing forces. Staying on course, staying committed to a task at hand, and applying the law of economy is one way to go.

Hard work implies putting in as much time as is necessary to a point of sacrificing if necessary in order to accomplish a set goal. Recognizing the value of the project, and seeing it through to its completion and doing it well.

Patience—with it you can endure setbacks, discouragements, temporary failures, rejections, disappointments, and when you fall you get back up, feeling stronger, wiser, better, more resilient to meet life's challenges.

Clear goal setting—without a clear goal, you will end up somewhere not intended.

A goal becomes a target of our perceived destination. On this trip to meet a goal, clarity of a goal makes us less wasteful of our time and energy in figuring out which way to go and what resources we may need to help us succeed. Clarity of the goal is a sure way to allow Divine Spirit to assist us toward the attainment of the goal. In essence, a goal is a mold we create. The clearer it is, the stronger the impression on divine spirit, the greater the divine forces are marshaled to help toward the achievement of the established goal.

The other vital element is motivation—without it, our efforts will lack the energy needed to move us forward, thus sooner or later we may fall flat on our face. And it becomes an arduous task to aspire to be the best that we can ever be. Without motivation from within, you will not go far.

We have to have enough love, liking, interest, ability, talent for what you choose to do, or it will be a stressful road ahead. A road to perdition with no joy, no satisfaction, no reward save for an empty monetary benefit if not all that is achieved. The price of pursuing something you have no interest or love for can lead to undue stress, which can impinge upon one's health and rob one of one's happiness.

The reverse is different. With right motivation, sincerity, self-discipline, hard work, right and clear goal setting, we are more likely to be more productive and lead a more fulfilling life. As such, the dividends go beyond monetary benefits. It becomes a life of fulfillment in more ways than one.

THE PURPOSE OF OUR EXISTENCE

The purpose of our existence is to make *God* a reality in our daily life, to enjoy life, and not just to endure it. God not as male or female, but God as the highest, all-encompassing, loving, neutral force from whence all life emanates, therefore, fittingly referred to as It, not he or she. The injustices that appear are merely a balancing of what we already put in motion; we caused them. And that is what is called Karma, for which there is good and bad. No matter how bad one's karma might be, it is not punitive, it is designed to teach us about love, freedom, and wisdom.

We can live a karmaless life by doing everything in the name of *God*. Instead of doing something for merely selfish reasons, we do it for *God*. The purpose of our existence is to manifest the God qualities lying latent in us. To grow in our awareness of who we are as conscious children of God. To recognize our divinity irrespective of our bank account, social standing, ethnicity, or age, or physical condition. To serve life selflessly. To cultivate our talents, interests, hobbies, and use them for the good of all and make life a joy to live for ourselves and others. To do the best we can under all conditions. To awaken to the fact that though our outer physical home may be sweet, it is indeed temporary and pales in comparison to our real permanent heavenly home.

Our true home is in the heavens, far beyond the lower heavens right into the pure God worlds, to the very hallowed home of God. So our purpose is indeed a noble one despite our humble outer conditions. And that is to realize and live an uplifting life, with a conscious knowingness that we are God's children and for that, we are eternally blessed and grateful.

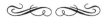

LOOKING GOOD FROM WITHIN

It sounds superficial when someone compliments another on how well, youthful or good the other person looks. But is it in reference to one's physical state, the outer physical temple? Or is it in reference to how positive one appears in a spiritual sense? If in reference to the spiritual side, implicit in that is that one may be magnetic, thus may have a positive disposition, aura, presence, vibes, or whatever you wish to call it. This implies beauty that transcends the physical bounds, coming from a place within one, from an inner core within our innermost self.

Therefore it is an inner radiance that is permeating through our entire being and yielding a good blending and coloring of one's outer physical self. In other words, an outflow of Divine Spirit permeating through one's physical beingness. A beingness characterized by love, an open heart, a loving heart,, an embracing heart, an unselfish heart, or a giving heart. With that as an integral part of our outlook, one will be looking good from within and without.

CYCLES OF LIFE

Life situations, experiences that are critical to our growth come in cycles. The end of one cycle often heralds the coming of a new cycle. The question is; if we have not successfully completed one cycle, does the new one begin? Or is it delayed till completion of an outgoing one, so can two cycles run concurrently. One whose eyes and ears are open may become aware of forewarnings or insights beforehand when a major cycle is about to start with prompts to start preparing for it so as to make smooth transition. Therefore, a new cycle may begin before the preceding one ends. For a new one is supposed to be built on the outgoing one.

They are not independent and isolated experiences, but more of a continuum.

Effective preparation, paying close attention to divine guidance, taking up necessary steps can result in a smooth transition through inevitable changes in one's life. So a certain level of flexibility is required whereby you are willing to let go of the past to allow in the new. With this type of attitude you will be able to transition more smoothly from one cycle to the next. Keep in mind that in due course, changes will happen anyway, but it is either you are dragged along if you resist the necessary changes or stay flexible and go along smoothly with the new changes ushered in by the new cycle.

TURNING ON A NEW LEAF

How do you turn on a new leaf so as to move forward in life? It is to our benefit to make time to fulfill our life goals. We think about the goals, plan them, but never seem to get time to follow through with them. We plan that we will start afresh some day, maybe next month, maybe at the beginning of the new year. But time never seems to come; we always find something else to do. Divine spirit has time and again showed us time to set new goals and start working toward achieving them. But time never seems to come. There seem to be not enough time. Yet there's always enough time to fritter away on unproductive things. There is always enough time to chill on the couch under the convenient belief that we need to rest, get some rest after a hard day's work even when we are not necessarily tired. Or sometimes we sit and think about what to do next instead of actually doing it. Before we know it, it's too late. Because we spent part of the free time brooding, planning, watching too much TV, making phone calls out of need to fill time. Kill time! By killing time, we are wasting an aspect of our valuable life.

It is in our best interest to attend to our talents, interests, hobbies instead of sitting around and doing nothing productive. Our valuable time goes underutilized, losing it, wasting it. We are left with nothing to show for the time spent in unproductive activities. Little or nothing is gained from unproductive activity or inaction. What is needed is a clear daily plan, daily recommitment to our life goals, doing them well and seeing them through to completion.

We can start with small manageable goals in the initial stages, progressing toward bigger goals and making adjustments as needed. Before we know it, we would have gotten where we set out to go and beyond if we let divine spirit guide us and we stay proactive. So it behooves us to move from planners to doers. With that, doors of new opportunities will begin to swing open. This is due to right action fueled by our selfless goals done for the good of all.

Let us change gears. Turn on a new leaf, waste no more time. If we plan our days and nights well, there will be enough time to fulfill our goals and some time left for leisure as well. Time well planned and spent is time well invested and enjoyed.

A SENSE OF CLARITY

Whether we know it or not, we all have a God given mission here on earth, small or big. Therefore it is incumbent upon us to find out what it is and work towards fulfilling it. Many people fail because they try to copy other people's dreams instead of identifying and pursuing their own. Where we are going is not always clear. Often we are going in all sorts of directions. What our goals are—our spiritual goals—we are not always sure. Often we set goals, if at all, that are influenced by fear, material gain, and sometimes we try to copy someone else's dream instead of pursuing our own. How to achieve the selfless goals, we're not always sure. Often we proceed in the most convenient way possible, with little effort, or in some instances so we can just to get by in life. The choices we make, are not always spiritually right. Often our choices are driven by material gain only, for most part. If we make choices that do not lead to a better place, to greater spiritual wealth, to a bigger room, they will leave us empty and unfulfilled. Keep in mind that there is nothing wrong with material sufficiency for it is part of God's plan. It is when materiality dominates our lives in such a way that our hearts close, rendering us unkind, unloving, cold and selfish that it becomes objectionable.

To proceed forward, to acquire true spiritual wealth, we need to learn to make right selfless choices, set clear goals and know where we are standing. We need a sense of clarity. In Divine Spirit, we will find clarity.

CHANGING TO WHO WE ARE TRULY

We appear to be many things in life save what we truly are. We may view and identify ourselves in any number of ways: weak, strong, angry, ignorant, stupid, intelligent, important, better than others, etc. But is that really our true nature or illusory nature or perception society has imposed on us or an image we have acquired from society? Whether we like it or not, we've become what we think we are and have internalized some of what others say and think we are. These various perceptions have taken root in our psyche. They have colored our lens through which we view the world around us and how we view ourselves. Thus our vision has been affected to the extent that we no longer have clear perception of who and what we are as Divine beings.

That is the danger of embracing borrowed perceptions and internalizing negative associations and letting them define us as our true identity and reality. To know who we truly are, to reclaim our true nature, we must let go of all old superficial identity, revise our wrong thought processes, recant our outmoded erroneous old beliefs of who we are and in so doing we will begin to chart a new course toward self awareness. We will begin to gradually awaken to that which is our true nature—*Soul.*

STAYING CONNECTED WITH THE ESSENCE OF GOD

To the extent that we are alive, the spirit of God exists in all of us, irrespective of differences in belief systems. It is what sustains our true identity as Soul.

It exists in the manner that you often don't recognize. Because you think yourself as merely this human being called by so and so name. Meaning your self-identity as emotions, mental and physical associations or outer Self. But you are greater than this. You are Soul to start with. You are Godlike in your true latent spiritual nature, a spark of God to put it more accurately.

When they say God is within you, that means the essence of God is within you. It's an aspect of you that rises above normal thought processes. That tells you what is right and what's wrong. That guides you to the right actions. That sends nudges to prod you to do something right, that may defy logic. However, nudges are not always easy to act on because they require an overcoming of self doubt and fear in order to do something that will take you beyond your comfort zone.

The more self-discipline you have in the ways of God without fear, the more of the spirit of God becomes an active part in your life. So, stay disciplined, seize the moment, rearrange your life in an uplifting manner and you will stay connected with the essence of God on a daily basis.

GETTING THE TRUTH
FROM DIVINE SPIRIT

In the outer we have certain human wants we seek so our lives are fulfilled, so we believe. We have concerns, fears, questions, that dog our lives. So, in seeking guidance from God, we ask with the backdrop of these underlying human wants, fears, passions, and anxieties. Therefore our quest for answers from God has built in expectations colored by the need to rid ourselves of these fears, or fulfill certain immediate human wants, understandably so. So that when answers come to us through dreams or our outer life, our perception is often influenced by our expectations of what we want. When they come in a way that does not seem to relate to our current condition directly, we don't recognize them so we disregard them and look the other way.

So, truth remains elusive and always unavailable to us and our endless questions appear to go unanswered. To get the truth, therefore, we should not expect anything, since God knows what we need better than we know at our limited mind level.

To get answers from God, it helps to stay open without expectations of how the answer will come. The attitude of expecting nothing yet expecting whatever divine spirit gives us is the best way to open ourselves to recognizing and receiving answers from God when they come.

LISTENING MORE TO THE VOICE OF DIVINE SPIRIT

Your assignment today is listening more to the voice of Divine Spirit. The more you listen, the more you can hear God's voice, and the more you know what guidance is coming from Divine Spirit. The more you can do what is needed to be done.

That itself is practicing the law of economy. Such actions, so in tune with the Divine Spirit, can help keep you connected with the Divine Spirit. You are in effect making God a reality in your day to day life.

So keep listening to that inner subtle voice of God. Till you reach a level where you don't do conscious effortful listening, but the voice of God is now heard effortlessly and naturally because your inner ears are trained. Our life becomes highly spiritual as we live more by the spiritual laws and within the spiritual laws.

With expanded awareness, we can hear more and clearer. Consequently, we can live our lives better. This is what learning to live in God is. Simply by learning to listen to the voice of God and following through with our actions. This does not mean you will always hear the voice the way you may expect it. God will communicate with you in its own way, on its own terms, through its own channels, sometimes subtle and covertly and other times overtly. Learning how to listen to God does not mean you will not make mistakes; you will, because making mistakes is part of growing. God may withhold something from you so you can learn by experience.

LOVING LIFE

Love is what makes you special as Soul. With this realization you will be filled with joy, beauty, inner peace and a profound sense of good will. You will begin to love life more because you see more beauty, more good, more love, more connectedness, more integration than before the realization dawned. It is to one's benefit to continually look to God for love. For love comes from God through all of us although expressed in varying degrees and ways to others depending on the nature of our relationship.

Realize that all living forms are created by God. Hence through loving God's creations, we get to begin to love God. Because each one is the same spark of God, it's an integral true part of God, God as Divine Spirit in action. This realization should help you change your attitude toward others. With this changed loving attitude, you are able to love God more. This is expressed through loving others, its creations, shown by the way you relate and treat them.

HOW CAN ONE LOVE GOD DAILY?

To love God to the fullest extent, one must totally submit to IT daily in order to re-gain the attained spiritual state. But the task for us is to learn how to weave this commitment minute by minute until it becomes effortless and organic. The key lies in one's ability to let go of all life. In letting go of all life, we are allowing God to step in. It sounds easy in theory, but its application can be challenging.

Think about it this way, when you let go of all things, only the things that are natural and beneficial to us spiritually stay in our lives, if anything, they come closer to us. This is so because the clutter of the unwanted material has been let go thereby creating room for what is needed. Life speeds up; life becomes spiritually abundant because every minute becomes transformed into moments spent in eternity, closer to God, in God's arms.

THE POWER OF LOVE

Love is what you need in order to have some measure of understanding about the inner workings of God. Love is what makes you become aware of who you are as Soul. Love does not stop you from engaging in life in a more passionate way. Love enhances your participation in life as it opens new avenues for greater and more adventuresome experiences.

Love heals wounds at the physical, emotional, or mental level, which may cause instability in one's life. Love is the key to an abundant life. Abundant, not necessarily in the material sense, but more importantly, in the spiritual sense. Spiritual is that consisting of wisdom, patience, kindness, respect, fairness, compassion, sense of sacrifice, and courage.

All these put together and made an active part of one's daily life makes for a remarkable spiritual human being. For love makes all things remarkable. Love in its Divine form has the power to transform one to an awakened spiritual individual, pulsating with love, connected to the essence of God. With pure love, one walks this earth while the heart lives in a joyous heavenly state with God above, making one an integrated spiritual human whole imbued with love, blessed by love, embraced by love and guided by love. So learn to cultivate this Divine love and your life shall be lifted beyond words.

NON-ATTACHED LOVE

To love God, is to have love. Love in this case meaning nonattached higher form of love that doesn't demand anything in return. Love that gives, gives, and keeps on giving. However, for it to be properly expressed, one must be selective. One must use discriminative powers to wisely give it where needed. Because it must be expressed, right action must be taken to manifest it. And action can take any form, such as simply listening to someone, helping someone financially, helping someone out of trouble.

There are numerous varied manifestations of higher love and their common denominator is in their truthfulness, selflessness underscored by a sense of nonattachment by the person giving out love.

To do a job well brings out qualities of excellence fueled by love. With love, the quality of the outcome of the deed becomes heightened. With love as the motivating factor, you draw in God's loving presence. Who better to be in charge of your life than God Itself. And with God as an active part of your life, your life will become an inspiration to others.

GOD'S ANSWER FOR YOU

When you have love in its divine form, you have the answer. The answer to unanswered questions. And also to unasked questions. The answer to unknown questions. The answer to all questions. The answer to life. The answer to all things. The deeper answer to known things. Known at a human level, but in an erroneous way. Now they can be known correctly from a spiritual perspective. From the perspective of Soul. From the higher viewpoint, the spiritual state. The unbiased and clearest viewpoint. From this vantage point, we can truly begin to know God. Then only can we consciously begin to express Divine love, and act out of love in the highest and truest sense of the word.

With love expressed this way, known this way, embraced this way, felt this way, you have God's answer to life—and that's Divine Love.

FULFILLING ONE'S WORK

To live a life of self-responsibility, ensure that you live up to what is expected of you in social, business and spiritual contracts. With such, you will be of service to life more than you would ever imagine. Doing all that you have agreed with others in some way is fulfilling God's contracts because It works through our actions, what we do, and how we conduct ourselves.

Through our actions, we bring God's spirit to bear. To keep our word aligned with requisite action is indeed to honor God. And it's our duty to do this: To finish off what you started and promised. Continue with what you set out to do, and you will live a life in harmony with the life around you and within you. With that, you will earn God's cooperation. This will come through your input, your diligent, and honest effort. Without the needed input from you, nothing starts, nothing goes anywhere. So, initiate the action and the flow of invisible forces will be activated, supporting your actions every step of the way. Leading to the eventual fulfillment of your set goal.

For what are we here for if not to become the best we can be in any chosen endeavor. Getting by is not enough if you wish to amount to anything of worth. Putting in your honest best effort, seeing a plan come to its completion is what counts. One who cares about what they do often wants to ensure that what they do is done well.

When something is done well, no matter how small the activity might be, it has the power to touch other people in ways that evokes and inspires love in their hearts. Such an act has a hand of God in it and those with spiritual eyes will see its impression on it and will have their hearts filled with love.

So, do well, finish what you start, and your life will be ever more enriching in measures beyond your expectations.

LOVE, THE KEY

Love in its pure and higher form is the key to unlocking the mysteries that confound us. The unlocking of the mysteries gives you insight into what exists behind the veil of illusion we are always confronted with. There are invisible forces that sometimes make their presence known through feelings or sensations without visible appearance. Sometimes we are faced with puzzles and unexplained circumstances that seem irrational yet have an effect, a real impact on our lives. We're sometimes faced with situations which seem not to have answers, logical answers at all yet have a real effect in our lives.

With expanded consciousness, therefore greater capacity for love, we are able to gain insight into these unfathomable and mysterious situations. Love, because it transcends the mind, the driving engine of logic and intellect. Love in its pure form, in its divine form lights up the dark alleys in our lives, opens up our inner eyes to enable us to view life more clearly.

Love not as we know it in the human state that imposes conditions on everything, but higher nonattached Selfless love expressed for the good of all.

ACTS OF LOVE

Since it is love that must be the key factor in your life, it should come first if you want to experience greater love. First, before all actions are considered, the factor of love must precede all you do. This is to ensure that your actions are fair, balanced and more productive. This entails taking time to do something with right discrimination and right amount of effort to accomplish it.

Act with conscious effort to tune in to the needs of the moment. In other words, learn not to rush through life for love never rushes. Do all in love's time. When missteps are made, realize that they are there to wake us up to greater love as we learn how to avoid a repetition of such violation. Mistakes and failures along the way are a part of the cosmic plan to teach us how to align ourselves with the law of love. Violating the law of love, repeating the same mistakes over and over only serves to set us up for a life of unnecessary suffering brought on by our failure to do the right thing.

It's through acts of love, consideration and fairness that our life becomes enriched, blessed with good fortune that gives us a greater sense of well-being.

CHANGE

Change is an inevitable and necessary part of growing and it implies moving from one state to another so we can move on in life as a new way unfolds before us. But often we resist change because we are fearful, misread the signs, and sometimes lack courage, understanding, and spirit of adventure. Often we are unaware of what our true spiritual needs are because our sight is not clear. Our sight is oftentimes clouded by our emotions and unconscious or willful ignorance. Emotions wrapped in chains of attachment to old loves, old values, old habits, and fears. Believing falsely that things should always be as they have always been. False peace, comfort zone, and familiarity trap us.

One cannot find true peace here on earth. One cannot find lasting comfort out here, so it's helpful to stop holding onto the way things have always been. One gets trapped by insisting on sticking to what's familiar only. In order for one to move on to greater awareness, one must not resist change. This way, one moves on in life, to new heights be it spiritual, material, or social. Not fearing going into areas we've not treaded before. Have courage in knowing that we are not alone; *God* is always with each one of us in one way or another. And with *God* in our lives, there's nothing to fear about change.

With right change, we grow in strength, wisdom, and more importantly, increased capacity to love more.

ELEMENTS OF LOVE

Love is what makes life change for the better. The elements of love are found in life situations that sometimes appear negative. This is the way things are sometimes set up so that only the pure in heart and mind would see beyond the illusion of negativity. You see good because you have good within your heart. You recognize love because you view life from the vantage point of your heart. You feel love because your heart is open to love. You love life because you embrace and face life with a loving attitude. You enjoy life because you recognize it's a gift from God.

When love comes into one's heart, things of the like nature are drawn to one.

Love opens new doors to new opportunities. These opportunities are windows for further advancement. These are opportunities for further growth, more love, more uplifting life experiences, which lead to a more fulfilling life.

LOVE IS THE KEY TO ALL LIFE

When selfless love enters your heart, your entire life changes. Life becomes a pulsating force that moves you along forward. Your life is no longer what it used to be.

It gets run in part by a higher power, a force greater than you, the essence of God. Thus your life becomes God-like in many respects. God-loving people who view life from the vantage point of their awakened, open hearts, will recognize it and become inspired by your living example.

You begin to walk on holly grounds wherever you go irrespective of outer conditions.

You become the center of activity and life moves to serve you. You begin to receive blessings where you didn't expect any. Therefore it behooves you to infuse yourself with love, make your deeds reflect love, and everything else will fall into place. With that, you will learn that love is the key to all life.

LOVING SELF AS SOUL, NOT AS EGO SELF

This relationship of God-child is what makes a child potentially possess higher love—the love for God. This is love beyond the little self, the ego self. The ego is the self that's most troublesome. Excessive love for the ego self impedes love for God. In other words, too much love for self diminishes the capacity for Divine Love in one's heart.

One needs to go beyond the little Self in order to be able to externalize love, to bring it out to the world through some modus operandi, often through one's talent, hobbies, interest, special ability, love given to another unconditionally.

God's love sustains all existing forms; it is externalized and at the same time internalized. The process of externalizing and internalizing love, strikes a proper balance between the inflow and outflow of love rendering one a balanced individual in one's daily life. One needs to love Self as Soul, not as ego, for it's by going beyond the ego that one is able to externalize love to the outer world. By so doing, you will grow in your capacity for more love.

LOVE CONQUERS TIME

Divine love is the only force that can take one beyond time, space, energy, and matter.

Because of its penetrative nature, it is the only force that permeates and creates a common link among all things that have life. For everything that has life is sustained in some way by love.

Divine love is the Godly force that makes one reconnect with God. And it is the only element that takes one to the land of beauty, Light and Sound.

Love is the only way to living in the moment. To live in the moment is to live in eternity, and to live in eternity is to live in God. God is the source of all life, so by living in God, you are living a life from the source of life, from whence love comes. Such a life becomes one that's of God, from God, with God, in God, beyond materiality of life, in the present moment.

Because God is present now with you, so be present for God for you to come into alignment with *It*. Coming into alignment attunes you to the nowness with God.

So, love realigns you to the moment, to the presence of God, to this very minute, so all your thoughts, actions, feelings converge and coalesce to this infinite moment, revitalizing the moment, actions become uplifting, feelings become joyful, life becomes ever more fulfilling.

LOVE: THE KEY TO SUCCESS

Love opens doors to a higher and more fulfilling life. Love for life is the key to doors of infinite opportunities. Love for what you need facilitates the fulfillment of that need.

Love for the things you wish to accomplish makes it easier to attain them. Love for people creates unity between you and others. Love for what you have makes you enjoy them more. Love for the gifts from God increases blessings in your life.

Living in moderation and Loving things you possess make you appreciate what you have more and help you value the significance of living within your means. Love opens your inner channels, so your higher inner consciousness gets integrated with your outer human consciousness. Once this happens, you will walk this earth an awakened Soul because your heart is now open to the music of God. With such an open heart, you are better able to embrace life greatly. And the gifts you recognize and receive are not only beneficial to you but also to others.

With the recognition of God's gifts, you can't help but be filled with gratitude. With a grateful heart, your heart gets filled with love for the miracle of life, the gift of life, the wonder of life and the joy of life. With *love* at the epicenter of all your actions, it paves the way to a better life and becomes the key to all success.

BROTHERLY LOVE

Since you are Soul, you must strive to reproduce the qualities of Soul in your daily life. When someone coined the word *Soul brother*, it seems it was done so out of need for unity. The truth of the matter is that Soul transcends race. That in Soul there's unconditional love. On the outer this catch phrase seemed to have racial overtone, yet it caught on because it had implications of brotherly love.

When you have love in your heart for another, irrespective of race, you are reproducing qualities of Soul. You are becoming a loving individual because you are manifesting the essence of God and making it a practical reality. So to bring out the Godly qualities, be loving to others and yourself. As you learn to see God in others, they will see God in you too. And what you become as a result of your obedience to God is what God intends you to be.

You become a reflection of the mirror image of God within the limits of your own individual consciousness.

GOD IS THE ESSENCE
OF ALL LIFE

God's design for each one of us is complex yet has a certain sequence and inherent order to it. At a social level, the complexity of life lies in the battle that ensues between the human social consciousness influenced by culture and tradition vis-a-vis with the inner Spiritual guidance. When this social conflict arises in rebellion against the inner dictates of Divine Spirit, man often succumbs to the social forces. Why? Because of the concern about the fundamental survival of human self.

In the human state, we are concerned with our image. Thus we put on an artificial façade to present to the public that is more praiseworthy. It, therefore, takes strength of character, courage, grit, and a great sense of self-honesty to face ourselves and follow the inner voice and carry through with necessary actions. This requires adopting a risk taking attitude that would catapult one above the social forces of conformity. To rise above all opposing forces is to answer the call from God, which leads to considerable achievement in one's life, spiritually and materially. In this state of spiritual triumph, one discovers that God is the essence of all life.

FACING LIFE

It takes courage to face life's challenges. In facing challenges, we avail ourselves the opportunity to face ourselves, learn, and grow. Yet how many times have we missed such vital opportunities? How many times have we avoided apparent difficulties because they didn't furnish us pleasure or we viewed them as inconveniences? How many times have we quit midway an undertaking that required special effort and patience which may have been the missing link? How many times have we refused to step out of our comfort zone to help a stranger in need? How many times have we had misfortunes we caused yet blamed everyone else but ourselves?

Life can sometimes be filled with challenges, but they are always for a purpose, never in vain, but placed there to help us grow even though it might not seem that way at the moment. Thus facing life and its challenges can be beneficial as it can be Illuminating, It's in facing challenges of life that we truly face ourselves. In so doing, we grow in our awareness of our true higher self—Soul self. So, let's pluck up some courage and face life's challenges that are put in our path. In so doing, we can avail ourselves of the vital opportunity to grow in our capacity for deeper understanding. With deeper understanding, fear is banished. Without fear, love comes in, with love, life expands and becomes a joy to live.

WHAT YOU GIVE TO LIFE, YOU GET BACK IN RETURN

The idea of getting back from life arises from the interplay between action and reaction. When you do something, whatever it is, it will at some point come back to you in equal proportion to the action. When you don't do something you are supposed to do, the energy flow will be suspended until conditions are set up again for a repeat of another opportunity. The next opportunity may come when we least expect it. It may be clothed differently. Thus it may sometimes take one's keen spiritual insight to recognize it.

We never get away from what we set in motion. This is the immutable law of action - you reap what you sew. The more actions we engage in, the more of a variety of experiences we have, the more of a variety of spiritual lessons we set ourselves up to learn. The less we do, the less we learn from life. Through life experiences, we learn what is right and wrong spiritually. So choose your actions, thoughts, and plans wisely for they shape your tomorrow and what life gives you in return and ultimately what you become. In the end, you realize nothing is ever lost, nothing is ever a waste, for life's lessons come from both bad and good circumstances. What is perceived as bad can simply be a missed lesson coming back for another chance to be learned.

What constitutes good is credit we reap for obeying Divine laws, and this makes for a more enjoyable and more forgiving life.

THE KEY TO LIFE

When Divine love is here in the now and you are open to it, you become love itself. It's in becoming love that you know who you are as Soul. You've this realization because you are instilled with innate ability to know directly the essence of love via Soul senses. When you know this via direct Soul understanding, you've unlocked the mystery to yourself. Once this problem of Self is understood spiritually, life as you know it changes. It may not change in the way it runs or unfolds, but may change in the way you view it. And as you change the way you view life, you naturally change the way you live your life. With this newly acquired ability, you are now able to see deeper into life, beyond illusion.

The illusion of life gets stripped away, making your life evermore authentic, without pretense, yet more engaging, more a part of a greater circle, because walls of illusion and negativity are now torn down.

Now what you see is an all-permeating force called love, the key to life.

DREAMING YOUR WAY TO SUCCESS

Dreams are an aspect of higher reality lived on the inner worlds that are in some way an extension of our outer existence. To that end, dreams can reveal truth that may be out of reach of the human consciousness. However, messages from dreams don't often come directly, they are often camouflaged in symbolism, sometimes they may appear topsy-turvy and may seem unrelated to our outer life. Hence it is important to listen to the dream messages carefully and watch for the symbols closely. Pay attention to whatever is going on in your daily life, big and small. For that may be a message from God to you to give you insight or reveal to you some aspect of your life that of which you need to be aware, thus give you better understanding and higher perspective about a situation in your life. It could be a message for you to carry out to improve your life so you can become a more spiritually alive and fulfilled person.

Whatever right guidance you receive from dreams, remember to apply yourself to the best of your ability in an ethical manner. It is your life after all, you want to make the best of it and live it well and fully. Always expect the best, and you will get the best sooner or later. Spirit expects the best. So why not you, since in essence, you are spirit-like; it behooves you to act in God's name. Dream your way to success by following your inner guidance whence your dreams originate.

To live in obedience to spirit's guidance is to succeed in living a life of spirit truly.

And there is no greater success, in essence, than spiritual success. So live it, be it, become it, and embrace it and all else will fall into place. This is so because true spiritual success encompasses all aspects of your life.

LETTING GO OF THE LOWER SELF

One way to come into closer relationship with Divine Spirit is to let go. Let go of all materiality that hold you in bondage to this world. In so doing, you allow control of your outer environment through self-will to be guided by divine will. In letting go of the control of our minds over our lives, we allow a higher power to take over control over our lives. This way, limitations of the mind that strive with abject failure to comprehend the unfathomable God are sidestepped, allowing Soul to use its higher spiritual faculties of perception, conception, and knowingness to understand higher spiritual truths. Thus, a greater power beyond our mind's ken and capacity can lead us to a higher and more direct road to higher planes of God. The taking over by a higher power brings corresponding new changes in one's life. One becomes increasingly more aware of the miracles that happen in one's life. Life becomes more fulfilling because the clutter previously weighing you down that took up valuable space in your life has been let go.

That is the power of letting go of the lower self to embrace the higher self that can lead us to a higher place, spiritually, that can in turn have a positive impact in our outer life.

LOVING THE OTHER AS SOUL

How do you love another person as Soul which you cannot see with human eye? You can start by giving them love without judgment, without bias, without thought of what they are, without thought of what they do, without thought of what they did in the past, without thought of how they look like, without thought of what they might do in the future. By so doing, you are bypassing the mind, the impediment to Soul if allowed to run uncontrolled.

By bypassing the obstacles to Soul, you are loving the other person as Soul so there is Soul to Soul connection.

It is Soul you should love and not anything in between. So loving without thought of anything in between is what loving another is in the spiritual sense even though you may dislike their actions. When you've accomplished this, you've made a small step yet a significant one toward the attainment of God knowledge.

ORGANIZING YOUR LIFE

At some point my life had gotten out of control, disorganized and I badly needed a change, some measure of order. So I contemplated on this and the insights I received were as follows: In order to move forward in an organized fashion, you must clear things up related to your business, social, and economic situations. It is important to stop and attend to these things or your life continues in a chaotic fashion. Organization entails, firstly, identifying problematic areas that need some order, then setting goals to address them. Goals that are achievable within a definite, specific time frame.

Organization helps one waste less time thus maximizes one's usage of time. It enables one to maximize ones resources with less effort. It allows the spirit of love to penetrate one's work. It brings order to what may otherwise be a disorganized time-wasting situation.

Disorganization is costly in terms of time and money. It can cost one missed deadlines, missed opportunities, missed due bill payments, and many other daily living responsibilities. Disorganization is the root of a life that's misdirected, wasteful, chaotic, and muddled. In this state, priorities get misdirected. Once order is instituted, life becomes a joy to live again. Things become easily accessible, work becomes more efficient, life becomes easier to handle, to run, to live again.

One can breathe again with relief, peace of mind, amid order. With an organized life, one can now stop and enjoy life a little more easily as things will now run a little more smoothly.

TIME HEALS

Life presents us with difficulties, problems, hard times that may sometimes leave us feeling hurt without any immediate remedy. Such harsh conditions may force us to wonder about the fairness and purpose of life. They make us stop to take a close look at life.

It helps to remember that these conditions are part of the continual life learning process. These adversities have a positive aspect to them, a silver lining, though it may not seem so at the immediate moment.

The choices we make today shape our future. They are correlated to the conditions we find ourselves in: good or bad. The truth is that we are responsible for our actions and inevitably the effects that arise from them. Oftentimes what stops us from doing the right thing is fear. There are different causes of fear: fear of other people's opinion of us, fear of offending others, fear of failing, fear we might not be good enough at something hence we dare not attempt something new, fear that something may be beyond our capability. Fear therefore, becomes a bane of our lives. However, be forewarned that fear may come under different guises, not easily understood or recognized at first glance, but may still have the same limiting impact in holding us from moving forward. And as long we let it dominate our lives, the price will be pain. Thus we will always need healing to regain our balance.

The reality of the matter is that when there is truth in what we do or say, done out of honesty and necessity with intent to do well for greater good, all will be well in the end. Sometimes the immediate effect may not be comfortable, because we are not always comfortable with the truth in that it makes us come face to face with our selves: our own shortcomings, our own human frailties. And once these shortfalls are exposed to others, we may look bad in the eyes of society. Hence we like to cover them up, so we present a more praiseworthy façade to the world. As if we had no imperfections, yet we live in an imperfect world. We forever grapple with it because society doesn't look kindly at our shortcomings. Hence we are forced to live a social lie. Once this lie is exposed, we resent it, get embarrassed, lose face or get hurt.

It would help to realize that nothing is permanent as long as this world of time, matter and space is concerned. Fortunately time can be a good healer. One ought to be patient to let time do the healing. So, it's best not to panic nor worry too much when we get hurt.

For later we may realize there was a valuable lesson to learn in the guise of pain.

With time, we heal and learn the purpose for the pain.

Time heals, but it takes patience and an open heart to discern the lessons for which the pain occurred.

MEETING CHANGE

Why is change so hard to face? Is it because it creates an atmosphere of uncertainty of what tomorrow may bring? Could it be because change demands a behavioral adaptation in order to meet new challenges? We tend to focus on change that takes place only in the outer and pay little attention to the inner. The truth of the matter is that real change of lasting value often takes place on the inner. Hence it's good to pay attention to night dreams. However, Inner change revealed through dreams needs to be approached and interpreted carefully because it can be open to a wide range of misinterpretations. For instance, if in the inner, you find yourself falling spiritually, this might indicate something not going right in some respect. Yet a cursory look at outer life may not show a direct relationship. This may cause one to miss the message the dream is hinting at. This may induce fear in one who doesn't understand this. And gripped with fear, It's easy to misinterpret the dream and consequently make wrong life decisions. Thus one needs to weigh inner experiences carefully. They could mean different things to different people. We shouldn't entirely trust the interpretation by someone else without careful consideration of the dreamer's prevailing circumstances.

Confusion in interpretation can make one stand paralyzed at the fork of the road, at a pivotal point in their life, unsure of what to do or which way to go.

Perhaps one may look to a spiritual guide or God for guidance as to which way to go.

A simple approach could be; God show me thy way, and invoke the proverbial prayer; *Thy will be done.* Thus making ourselves receptive to God's guidance.

With *God's* hand in it, change may be met more easily with confidence.

GOING BACK TO THE WAY THINGS USED TO BE

Often we hesitate, trip, fall, doubt ourselves, fear when change comes about unexpectedly. We find ourselves in unfamiliar territory where the pace is faster than our usual pace. Unaware that this could be a new opportunity to learn, to grow, to enrich our lives. Yet we become overcome with self-doubt. We feel we are not ready. Hence a need to go back to the way things used to be begin to tag on us—frozen in our tracks, unable to move forward. The inner nudge egging us to move forward, it's the inner call of Soul urging us to move on toward our destiny - known or unknown. Not wanting to give up the outmoded old ways, we resist change. This inner conflict tears us apart. We become our own inner battle ground. Not knowing which way to go, to take a risk and step into unexplored territory or stay safe in our familiar environment? Often we choose to be safe in our familiar environment, unknowingly stay trapped in the limits of our own perceived safe cocoons. By choosing to be safe and stay within the restrictive walls of false safety, we unknowingly or knowingly turn away from growing and awakening to higher truth. Higher truth that tries to elevate us to the next higher level, often stretching us beyond our comfort zone.

The voice of fear, by its inherent nature turns us away from higher truth.

It's our duty to confront it and conquer it so we can reclaim our journey toward exploration of higher truth. It behooves one not to heed the voice of fear. Fear serves to stop us in our tracks and points us back to old familiarity—to the way things used to be.

We fall for this because most of us don't want truth for it places us in unfamiliar territory. Yet that's the nature of truth and its power to lift us to our higher grade of ourselves once we discover it and embrace it. By its nature, it is always that which we are not familiar with once we acquire it.

So how do we find truth if we always turn away from it once the opportunity presents itself? If we only seek what's familiar, we may never find truth. Let us not revert to the way things used to be. Let's learn to give up the old in order to accept the new. And march on ahead, deeper and deeper into the heart of truth. For in there lies the essence of life, the life that keeps beckoning us to move forward to our destiny.

ATTITUDE

Our attitude, in many ways, can be shaped and influenced by how others treat us. Attitude toward ourselves and others go hand in hand. How we see ourselves colors and influences how others see us, thus treat us. If we think we are not good enough, we will transmit an aura of one with a lack of confidence. If we think or feel we don't deserve something, by our own inner rejection, it will be kept at bay from us. If we don't respect ourselves, others will not respect us. If we believe that we can't have something, we may not have it. We may have it partially, but not completely. Because the heart has to first accept the gift completely before it can be ours fully.

We let ourselves be treated in proportion to the way we treat ourselves based on our own attitude and our perception of ourselves and others. If we extend respect to others, the world will in turn respect us. Our very presence will yield a sense of trust and respect from others. We will become an inspiration to others if we conduct ourselves in an ethical manner.

Everything is contingent upon our own perception of ourselves and others. The more we have a positive outlook of ourselves and that of others, the more others will see us in a positive light. So let's examine ourselves and determine what attitudes need to be changed and matched with our new values so our relationship with life can be more positive. Just remember it's all about attitude. Examine it, reshape it to the positive results you want to evoke from life, and your relationship with life will change for the better.

REACHING A GOAL

Sometimes one wonders whether all the effort we put in achieving something is worth it. We do what we can to accomplish something or reach a goal. When the going gets tough, our human natural tendency is sometimes to quit. We quit because we may lack self discipline, we may have fear, we may lack foresight and insight, or lack courage, or patience to withstand the tests of time. We may feel we've spent too much time to come up against a seemingly dead end. Is it really a dead end or is it just our misperception of it? Did we correctly read all the signposts leading up to this? Were they negative or positive signs?

Did we understand them?

Incorrect understanding of the signs along the way may lead us in a wrong direction thus cause us anxiety and fear. If we want instant gratification, we may become impatient, thus rush and fail to read the signs correctly;

therefore, stumble and fall. This impatience has harmful effect in as much as it may lead to unnecessary mistakes, failures or frustrations. Some may panic. Panic may scatter the energy we so desperately need to keep the goal in focus and alive. It would make us close in on ourselves. Closing the aperture which the divine nourishment is supposed to come through to sustain our spiritual energies.

Without sustained effort, we are doomed to fail. We need an open heart, receptive to divine intervention in order to ultimately reach our selfless goals.

When we ask divine guidance to help in the fulfillment of our goal, we should also wish the same for others. It's a way to stay selfless in our attitude and actions. If we act selfishly, we are liable to fail spiritually and our success if any will be limited, empty and unfulfilling as it will not be for the greater good.

Patience is an important factor that can go a long way in helping us move steadily toward reaching our goal. It's helpful to realize the importance of cultivating the virtue of patience in all things we do. A lack of patience can cause one to rush and easily stumble and fall. It is when we rush that we make most mistakes. Too many mistakes can cause us to create more obstacles for ourselves, thus jeopardize our goal achievement. We need patience in order to achieve anything of worth. Absolute patience must be a virtue we must all learn to live by. With patience, we safeguard ourselves against premature quitting as we endeavor to pursue our goals. We have to learn to steadfastly hang on despite discouragements and setbacks along the way. With such disciplined steadfast attitude, we can reach any goal of worth that is aligned with our destiny.

DOING EVERYTHING YOU HAVE AGREED TO DO

There's wisdom in following up with all that you have agreed to do which can involve the agreements with your clients, friends, family, strangers, coworkers or whoever with whom you enter into agreement.

Every agreement fulfilled leads to strengthening of trust, friendship, unity, harmony between parties involved. And, every agreement breached, may cause the opposite effects such as distrust, dishonor, hostility, ill feelings, or disharmony. So do what you have agreed to do so your life is that of integrity, promise, and honor.

There are not many people of honor and integrity in the world. Many people put on a façade of personal integrity that they present to the public yet deep down within their inner being, their secret thoughts tell a different story. Strive to be one of the numbered few with integrity.

This world can use a few more of this caliber. The world can be lifted in many respects with such an uplifting approach to life. Engage life from a position of truthfulness, trust, honesty and life shall never repay you negatively. You will win friends, associates, restore broken relationships. Your life will be a reflection of high personal integrity.

With integrity, you will be the go-to person because people can trust you.

Such is the power that lies in honoring your agreements.

FINISHING THINGS PENDING

Life provides us with endless opportunities for spiritual advancement. If your heart is open to truth, you will note that there's a spiritual gem embedded in each activity. If you can recognize that, you are increasingly living in the consciousness of Divine Spirit. Meaning, conscious of God's presence. These are things that make your spiritual eyes ever keener and clearer. It is this keenness that makes you a spiritually aware and awakened person.

When we start an act and leave it unfinished, the flow of divine spirit which was giving sustenance to that act is cut off. Cut off as long as we don't resume that activity.

So learn to finish things once started unless divine spirit steers you in another direction.

It is a spiritual discipline to finish off things we started. It's like starting a journey and stopping midway, it's wasted energy, effort and time. We are not learning by quitting prematurely. Lessons are thus left unfinished. Once needed lessons are left unfinished, this will come back to hurt us in some way on our journey home. We may suffer unnecessary pain in some way commensurate to an unfulfilled goal.

So learn to finish off pending things so your life can run more smoothly as you will be able to meet the future in a more prepared manner.

LOSS IS GAIN

Loss presents a paradox. In losing something, we may suffer a sense of deprivation, yet we may gain something valuable in turn--a blessing in disguise.

An affair ending may create a void, pain, and emotional suffering. A part of one seems to die and momentarily the future may look bleak. Sometimes we let ourselves feel we can't go on without the person. These are moments when Soul is tested. Tested often in areas of weakness. This is when we let our emotions cloud the positive influence of Soul upon our human consciousness.

What this means is that these are areas that need working on, polishing, strengthening, and gaining maturity. It is in these areas we need to develop spiritual and emotional stamina to deal with them. Once we deal with them successfully, we can move on forward. However, bear in mind that what's easy for one maybe hard for another person. So it is best not to judge another who is going through difficulties. Sometimes only time and patience enable us to heal and learn lessons that seem hidden within our losses.

On the other hand, in losing something, we may be eliminating a spiritual obstacle. In losing something that is outmoded, we may be creating room for growth, for something new. This way we can awaken to a new state and embrace a new you with new, higher values. In this case loss becomes gain.

SPIRITUAL RESOLUTION TO A BUSINESS IMPASSE

Everything you do must be geared toward allowing spirit to flow through to restore balance. When there is an impasse, it means the two sides are not agreeing on issues in question. If you are on the side of spirit, you will let God guide you so that what is spiritually necessary is done with love. Leaving situations unresolved cuts off the flow of spirit.

Learn to act on issues with integrity, honor, and respect for another. Never act out of anger, vengeance, or to get even. When you recognize your role and mistake in something, acknowledge it to the other, make peace. When you see a mistake, try to point it out to the other if it's true and necessary but be respectful. When you are able to do all actions with love, consideration, and fairness, the defensive walls of anger and spite will break down. A new pathway to where a solution becomes possible again will be forged. What seemed impossible now seems possible. What seemed problematic becomes manageable. What seemed difficult becomes easier. What seemed bad becomes good. What seemed a stumbling block becomes a stepping stone. And with that, an impasse becomes solvable.

A PRAYER OF THANKS

It is a day to give thanks. Thanks for life. Thanks for what went on before us.

Thanks for what America is today with all its blessings. Today's America is verily a product of failures and successes of yesteryears. Today's state of liberty of USA is an offspring of past struggles, trials, and tribulations. Difficult times that served to render human spirit stronger and ready for a renewed more prosperous America.

It is in this spirit of recognition of such acts of valor that led to the America we enjoy today that we owe an eternal debt of gratitude. Thus to give thanks to what spawned the freedom we enjoy today is to honor the forefathers of this beloved land.

Look to God and say a prayer of gratitude. For all that represents freedom and independence has in some way been touched by the hand of God. So that the freedom we enjoy now is to a great extent the freedom bestowed on us from God through human effort, struggle, and sacrifice.

Enjoy the day, break bread with your family and friends particularly the beloved ones close to your heart. And bless this day.

THE ACT OF LOVE

When you perform actions driven by love, they have a tendency to open closed hearts through which love connects with those for which the act is intended. But it has to be the right action which acts as a conduit for love. Thus a wrong act can unwittingly lead to less love. So to truly love, you must truly act with love. You do so by giving of yourself honestly to the other person. You must do it unconditionally without expecting anything in return.

The act of love, if pure and unconditional will move the other person to act in the manner that fits their own way of doing things. So that you don't have to expect the same act in return. If you offer to give your love to someone and you get no response, don't be disappointed. Simply accept conditions and let them play out their natural course without forcing issues and without expecting anything. Keep in mind that a good act lives forever. Love moves in its own way at its own speed; you can't force it, can't rush it, you can't manipulate it. It operates best in an environment of freedom and mutual trust. In that environment it is bound to thrive and flow uninterruptedly and in greater abundance.

THE PAST RESURFACES

The past has an uncanny way of resurfacing. It often resurfaces because we still hold onto certain outmoded and unworthy thoughts in our minds. That means recreating situations of which we wish to get rid. Forgetting that life always moves us forward. Life always gives us new opportunities to explore. Life presents us with new situations for us to experience.

When something new happens in our life, sometimes it is to inform us that it is time to move on and let go of the past. Sometimes it is telling us to let go of something or someone we may be too attached to so we can move on. Firstly, we must free those thought processes from our minds. As long as we harbor them, we are also holding onto that situation or person in time. So free yourself and let go of such so you can move on, and the other person can move on too. Otherwise we may be inadvertently placing a psychic block on ourselves and them, stopping them from moving forward or stopping a situation from running its natural cycle. The natural rhythm and direction of life is forward movement. For us to move forward and in synch with life we have to allow others to move on. Because life always moves us along to new experiences. Don't hold onto what was and no longer is. Lest the unfavorable aspects of our past we are trying to leave behind resurfaces. Thus hold us back and repeat the old undesired experiences over and over again.

PAINS OF AWARENESS

In knowing something you are not prepared for, you are liable to get hurt. Yet we always want to know the truth so we are not cheated. Our hearts hurt when we find out we are cheated. Why? Because the trust was betrayed. It becomes harder for us to love and open our hearts again lest someone abuses it. Soon we learn that there is safety and advantage in knowing but also with it comes a price of pain if not ready for it. Pains of knowing may arise from a lack of understanding. A lack of understanding may stem from closed consciousness. Closed consciousness may be born out of a lack of proper spiritual tools by which one may gain enlightenment. With enlightenment comes proper understanding of the harsh realities of this life. With understanding, pains of awareness will be assuaged. This makes our day to day challenges of life a little easier to handle. Despite pains of awareness, it is helpful to remember that such harsh realities of life are designed to make us stronger, wiser, and more loving.

Pain is temporary but the wisdom we gain from it may serve us well in the future.

Thus it works to our advantage as it becomes part of our life survival skill. We gain a life skill for our future life battles. Equipped with a new survival skill, we become ready to take on new life challenges of tomorrow.

THE PARADOX OF THE VOICE OF *GOD*

The language of *God* is truth, always truth. Yet we are often uncomfortable with the truth? Are our minds schooled in the art of receiving God's truth? Are our minds tuned to higher truths that come from God? Are our minds capable and equipped with senses to recognize God's voice? The way of the mind is not the way of the eternal voice of God. The mind is too limited to recognize the voice of God in its fullness. So when God speaks, the mind limits the message to what it can handle. Thus the message received, if at all, is limited, modified and lowered to the mind's level. The mind by nature is limited and in its willful blinded awareness enjoys control of one's life. Everything seems to pass through the mind, gets processed through our minds, and then passed on to our human state.

When *God* speaks, we tend to listen with our minds through the filter of logic. But God's message comes from a source beyond the reaches of logic. Hence all we receive is filtered and distorted messages that are forced to conform to logic. When *God* lights up the way so we can avoid the snares from the negative force, our logical eyes are too limited to see. So we misconstrue the messages coming from up above, thus receive incorrect information, which then guides our lives in a wrong direction. This may cause us to trip and fall and hurt ourselves. We cry and wonder why *God* didn't prevent this from happening.

Sometimes *God* takes away something we may be too attached to, but that may serve as an obstacle to our growth. If we place undue attachment to that object and have a false dependency on it for our survival, we often resist, fight tooth and nail out of fear and ignorance, without realizing this could be a blessing in disguise. This could be a crutch we need to get rid of but unable to recognize it for what it is because our inner vision is blind and we are deaf to the ways of God. Yet we wonder why *God* doesn't help us and give us guidance in affairs of our life when it is us who are resistant to its impeccable guidance.

When *God* continuously gives us love, our heart is often closed to receiving it.

As a result we complain and wonder why *God* does not love us. This is the paradox of the voice of *God* which is constantly speaking to us yet we do not hear its perfect liberating message, Its impeccable guidance, because we are too dependent on the mind whose logical nature runs counter to the voice of *God*. It behooves us to learn to rise above the mind so as to open our eyes and ears so we can begin to hear and see God's messages as they come to guide us in the right direction toward our destiny.

LIFE GUIDED BY LOVE

YOU ARE AN ASPECT OF GOD

How do you fully awaken to what you are as an aspect of God, which is Soul, to become Self realized ? The process is not easy and it is beyond the scope of this book. But you can start by listening to God within you, carefully without fear, without bias, without conditions, without prejudging, and without expectations of what God may say. Bear in mind that: God is love. Love is God. You are love. Love is the essence of all life. To live life with love is to live life with God. To live life with God is to live life fully. To live life fully is to fulfill your destiny. By fulfilling your mission, you are indeed answering the call of Soul. To clearly answer the call of Soul, you must disregard the call of the ego-self. To do so, you must put your ego self second and Soul Self first in order to act as a clear instrument of God.

So surrender to God to receive guidance toward the fulfillment of your mission.

Each one of us has their own God given mission. Once we recognize it and work toward achieving it, this becomes a gift to the world designed to uplift.

In your endeavor to become a conscious aspect of God, let GOD be with you as your daily protector, comforter, guide, and teacher on your journey toward your destiny, toward awakening to who you are as a conscious aspect of God.

WHEN LOVE COMES,
LIFE BEGINS ITS ASCENT

Love is the highest force that truly builds life. Though invisible in its existence, it can be felt, lived, manifested through action. Action born out of love is enduring; it transcends the physical act in its quality and impact. Love if allowed to be the force behind any action, has uplifting influence on all that it touches. It's this type of love coupled with courage that moves people, communities, and nations to a higher level and to move forward. It's this type of love that breaks barriers that hold people captive within a certain confined level of social, political, and even economic consciousness. It is love, that inner God impulse that moves you to act out of selflessness. It is love that sustains you through periods of turmoil, apparent failure, setbacks, and discouragements.

It is love that drives you to help others in need. The love that is fair, kind, considerate, yet firm in its course in bringing about positive changes. It is love that drives you to live life in higher planes of consciousness while here on earth. So that though you are in this world, you are truly not of this world. Because with love in your life, your heart lives in the heavens while lending support to your outer life and actions.

BECOMING A CONSCIOUS GOD CHILD

When you have awakened your consciousness, certain hidden facts of life become clearer and evident. Facts of life which are spiritual truths that are hidden from the profane eye. Facts that are only gained through purification of one's consciousness. The spiritual facts gleaned from the inner higher God worlds that are nonphysical thus cannot be proven to anyone save those whose spiritual eyes are open.

They can be experienced directly through spiritual senses. This is so because they are of spiritual nature and cannot be comprehended by someone who does not have the requisite spiritual awakening.

Everybody has these inner higher truths locked away behind the veil of illusion.

Everybody is Soul, yet not many know who they truly are. Love is the key element that begins to open the window to the qualities of the inner Soul self. Love is the key that allows the ego Self to yield to the higher Soul self.

And it's this awakening to the Soul Self that leads to the gradual understanding of who we are as conscious children of God.

WHEN YOU LOVE UNCONDITIONALLY, LOVE COMES BACK TO YOU A HUNDREDFOLD

With unconditional love as a gift to others, it opens their hearts and in turn yours. With an open heart, life around you changes. Your life may change in unexpected ways but always for the better. Oftentimes these changes may elude you. They may be so subtle as to go unnoticed. Yet their impact in your life may affect you in ways that may be real and life changing. In ways that may open your heart and others through your actions rooted in love.

Some people may feel your presence and become acutely aware of you. Some may feel drawn to you and may enjoy your company. People may feel something about you that makes you tick but may not place a finger on it. Others may want to know you and associate with you. Because love has this power to touch other Souls in a unique and special way. In a way that will light up others and infuse in them a sense of joy, hope, and beauty.

Love has the power to heal, to create better conditions for you and others.

The other advantage of unconditional love is that it has the power to break down walls of hate, discrimination, and illusion in the fullness of time.

OPENING YOUR HEART
TO MORE LOVE

When you begin to open your heart, love begins to flow more spontaneously, without forcing it. This takes effort to let love flow effortlessly. This is so because it takes effort to learn how to discipline our thoughts. The way you look at things must change. In other words, you must listen more to the inner voice of God. Then let this voice become your viewpoint from which you view life. This takes proper attitude of surrender of your thought processes to allow Soul and its innate higher spiritual faculties to come into the foreground. In other words, surrender to God your limited ideas of running things. And allow new higher spiritual ideas to be in charge of your inner being, in charge of your inner self, in charge of your thought processes as much as is practically possible.

This is not easy to do, but once accomplished, you will rejoice in a state that no one else would understand. So listen more to the inner voice and the voice will guide you to what you need to do. Just be aware that the guidance may come in many varied ways, such as a nudge, intuition, insight, hunch, inner gentle voice or knowingness without recourse to the mind.

The act of listening itself opens your heart because it is a form of surrender to God.

By surrendering to God, you allow more love to come into your heart.

DIVINE SPIRIT, MY TRUE FRIEND

Life sometimes plays its hand in ways that can leave us astounded yet reassured. It reveals its minutest of secrets when our hearts are open. It shows us guidance, gives us hints through dreams, golden tongued wisdom, waking dreams, all intended to help us along the way through the vagaries of life. And this life revealing force that confides in us is Divine Spirit. It's like a friend, a true and trusted friend that is always there through thick and thin.

The more we trust it, the more It trusts us, and the more we work in harmony with It. The more we keep its secrets, the more it confides in us.

It's the only friend I know whose friendship is based on true abiding mutual trust. To maintain this vital, nurturing relationship, I must trust It implicitly at all times. It's the only friend I know who will never fail me under all circumstances. When I am hungry, it's there to give me the nourishment I need. When I am in grief, it's there to bring me comfort and hope. When I am lost, it's there to show me the way. When I am fired from my job, it's there beside me showing me a way to another job. When I fall, it's there to pick me up. When I have lost hope, it's there to restore in me a sense of hope.

All it demands of me is that I trust *It*, open my heart to *It*, listen to *It*, and learn to live in harmony with *It*.

YOUR RELATIONSHIP WITH GOD

In what way can you establish a stronger relationship with God? Start by remembering that God from whence Divine love issues, sustains you through love. Love is the stuff of spirit. Divine love is what supports life, life in whatever form it manifests itself. Partaking in it always leads to an expansion of life, an abundance of life, and a life of self sufficiency.

The abundance of life lies in how much you have love in your life. The quality of your life is predicated on how much of truth is the foundation of what you do, what you say, what you think and believe. Without truth, you've no life of integrity. Without truth, you have no light to guide you in the right direction. Without truth, you live in the dark while all along you believe you live in the light.

Love begets life. Life begets circumstances that bring about new opportunities for further advancement. Life as we know it must be lived in truth, in spirit, and in fullness.

It's in living life in fullness that God supports you in fullness because God helps those who help themselves. So remember to embrace life so life can return its embrace.

Once you embrace life with love, life must support you, for God always returns the favor a hundredfold, and your relationship with God will gradually start to become stronger.

THE DAILY PRESENCE OF GOD

How can one learn how to live in the daily presence of GOD? You can start by slowly giving up your base desires by taking away too much attention off of them and placing more attention on one single object, the highest one—God. Strive to place all your strength and hope in this singular factor, remain steadfastly positive, faithful, and trusting so as to stay connected to the everlasting presence of God. This yields a partnership that is unfailing that can help us withstand all pressures that aim at breaking our focus so as to break this inner link. This requires steadfast trust that is undiminished when all is falling apart around you. Once one gets well grounded in God, it gets easier to maintain the inner link with God under all conditions. For it is only the *God* in action—expressed as Divine Spirit, which you should lean upon. This is the only God force that will help you even when you no longer need it. This God force shall stand by your side when everyone else is letting you down. It will carry you on its wings when you are tired, weak, and weary. This force of love will always give you love unconditionally even when you are unable to requite it.

To recognize, honor, and maintain this partnership as much as practically possible is to consciously live in the daily presence of *God*.

SIMPLY BE

We are continually trying to seek answers to life. In an attempt to do that, we either consciously or unconsciously try to use and direct the Divine Spirit to fulfill some need in our life. Sometimes we want to know the right action to take. In an effort to do that, we may ask *God* to show us the way. Yet in asking we may be inadvertently trying to dictate the outcome to God. We are in actuality asking *God* to show us the way that is convenient to us. In other words, our way.

It is easier and tempting to seek the right way according to our will not the right way according to Divine will.

By placing our will, first and, Divine will second, we are using Divine will in reverse. This is a wrong way to work with divine spirit.

The right way is to let divine spirit use us. We adjust our lives so we do everything according to divine will. But often in our effort to harmonize our will with divine will we err by trying to bend and reduce this higher will to conform to our terms, which are often of a selfish and limited nature. A first step in the right direction is to learn to listen to the voice of *God* without predetermining the outcome. Resisting to listen to the self-righteous and egotistical voice of the mind. This way we steer clear of psychic entrapments and mind stuff.

In an effort to know where we are going, we always somewhat want to know the future. What drives us to do so is an underlying fear, anxiety, impatience about tomorrow. To do all in accord with Divine Will, all we have to do is relax and *simply be.*

HELP FROM GOD

God may initiate rendering its help by showing you in some way what needs to be done. It's this realization that enables you to start the initial effort to move forward. When you act upon God's guidance, you are doing for God what can only be done through you. You are in essence acting on behalf of God.

When this happens, you are lifting the world consciousness ever so slightly to a new height. The purpose of all this is to grow in recognition of how God works through you, with you, and for you. If you can recognize this process and work with it on a regular basis, you and others will notice that your life will change over time. Things around you and your perception of them will change.

People and animals alike will respond to you and look at you differently. Some people will seek your company if Divine Spirit determines it is needed for a purpose. So be watchful for that hand of God because it may come when least expected. Be alert, be vigilant; so when God speaks, you will recognize its eternal voice. And your life will evermore be guided to the right places, right conditions, and to the right people.

UNLOCKING GOD'S TREASURES

With unconditional love, you get anything you need that will benefit the universal cause. Love at its deeper level is the God force that is unconditional. But once conditions are placed on it, Its unhindered flow gets blocked commensurate to the type and degree of blockage. A vague echo and tainted love is what becomes manifest in one's life. To avoid this, strive to love without conditions and the world will open its treasures to you. If you love with conditions, the world will deny you of its true wealth, the heavenly more superior wealth that you can never put a price on. So it behooves you to learn to love without conditions and you will become a living, pulsating magnet of love.

Life will be centered around you and all things necessary for your growth will begin to align themselves to serve you. Yet in truth, it is because you are serving life. You are forever giving life to all around you. This is the key to love. This is the way to becoming love itself.

Trust in God, for It knows what you need and with love in your heart, God's treasures will await you till you are ready to receive them.

YOU ARE SOUL

We are Soul in actuality. But we don't know because our vision is blinded by the allures of the material world. Our outward focus renders us blind. Blind to our higher spiritual nature. Blind to our true essence. Blind to our Divinity. Blind to our higher reality. Blind to our true mission. But there are few that muster up enough courage, self honesty, and moral strength to look within for who and what they are.

There are those who listen for the inner voice. This inner voice if not listened to, grows fainter and fades into silence. Some people have the purity of heart to hear the inner voice of God that continually speaks to us when we are ready to listen in.

Most of us don't hear it because we are too caught up in the outer world of materiality.

So stop for a moment, listen to the inner voice, this will begin to open you to divine love and through that you will gradually know who you are as Soul.

LIVING A LIFE OF DIVINE SPIRIT

Living a life of divine Spirit means many things yet one thing; To live in the spirit of love. One can start by giving up one's habitual negative thought patterns and surrendering oneself into the loving arms of God.

Let us learn to let go of strong negative or outmoded opinions for they have a tendency to form pockets of negative energy that in turn stands between you and the love of *God*. To practice detachment, to trust fully in the guidance from *God* even though it may not conform to logic and be outside our comfort zone, to not judge situations but let them be viewed for what they are from a spiritual perspective, to be patient in all things good and bad so we don't overlook life's lessons so as to stay balanced and not be swept off by phenomena, to not seek possessions in the outer but truly in the inner, is indeed to live a life of divine Spirit guided by love. By so doing, you'll be allowing God to be the invisible driver in our lives, minute by minute. And day by day.

PASSING THE GIFT

God gives us gifts for the upliftment of the universe. Whatever you partake in, if it is from *God*, it multiplies. If from self, born out of the passions of the mind, such as undue attachment, anger, vanity, lust, greed, it diminishes the more you give it out, leaving you ever more impoverished. If it's from *God*, you receive it and keep it to yourself for a selfish purpose and self glorification, you impose limitations on it and on yourself. Soon you become overfilled, and no room left for more gifts to come through from God.

As you give and receive, you grow in your capacity to store more, receive, and give more love. Your universe can't help but expand in all aspects of your life. You will be able to touch more Souls. Your role, therefore, is to identify gifts which issue from *God*. Once identified, partake in them, share them, and by so doing, you're truly serving God and living in the presence of *God*. So pass on the gifts, don't hoard them in some hidden dark hole. They don't belong in hidden places where no one sees them save you. They belong to the universe. They are for the enrichment of all including yourself and others.

ALLOWING IN DIVINE SPIRIT'S INFLUENCE

There are many ways we can knowingly or unknowingly block the positive Iinfluence of Divine Spirit in our lives. Thoughts, beliefs, attitudes, expectations at mind level serve to block the Soul and cater to the mind. To let go of the hold on these thoughts which are often earthbound opens a door to allow the Divine Spirit in. This happens by persuasion, not by force of one's will. It happens by total implicit trust in Divine Spirit. With this release on our thought processes, we enter a world of real spiritual action. A world removed from one dominated by actions born out of self-interest directed at serving the ego. Now we enter an expanded world of real spiritual wealth, filled with heavenly music of God. It's a world we should aim to live in for it brings into our lives love, beauty, joy, wisdom, strength, depth of perception, and greater insight into our daily life's problems. With this, life becomes a joy to live and has a deeper meaning than before.

LISTENING TO THE INNER VOICE OF *GOD*

By listening to the inner voice of God, you will begin to know what needs to be done and that which shouldn't be done. What's illusion, and what's not. What's truth, and what's not. What's love and what's not. What you should avoid, and what you shouldn't. What is good music for you, and what's not. What good food to eat, and what's not. By listening to God, you will receive the best guidance ever. Your life will have meaning, purpose and direction. So, listen up! Listen in! Listen for the inner nudge!

It's God speaking!

ENGAGING IN ACTIVITIES THAT WILL EXPAND YOUR LIFE BEYOND WHERE YOU ARE

Activities that will open new avenues for further advancement are worth engaging in. So it behooves one to go out and participate in them. Go out and engage in society's activities that have potential to open your heart to God. Often these are activities you love to do or have a special ability for or interest in. Once you participate in them, you bring God's love into action. So you must cherish them and engage in them with love. Without love, it doesn't matter what you do. With love, even if you do a small act, it multiplies in effect at different levels. So be selective in what you do for it will determine how far and deep you will go in life.

Choose what you love to do mainly. This will open your heart with less effort than if you were to choose something you had no interest in. If you choose to pursue a career you don't love or have no interest in, you will sweat, toil, unnecessarily suffer to achieve measurable success. And even when the goal is achieved, it will be an empty achievement for what good is getting something you have no love for? It may only serve to cause you stress, heartache in the long run. Before long, you will start looking for something that may provide you joy, something that will open your heart as you engage in it. It's Soul's nature to do so, to express its expansiveness in all it engages in as long as it serves as a conduit for love. Hence it is advisable that one chooses activities that conduce to expanded expression of Soul. For it is through the expanded consciousness that we better serve and embrace life in its higher degree.

And our life will no longer be a limited and self-involved one but one that becomes selfless, more loving, happier, dynamic, and more engaging.

LISTENING TO DIVINE SPIRIT AND FOLLOWING IT WITHOUT QUESTION

When Divine Spirit guides you to do something, follow it. The things that get revealed to you are for your own spiritual benefit. Honor them, follow through with them. It is what you are supposed to be doing. That's the key to living a spiritually active life. Through these insights, you are led to do something greater and more spiritually fulfilling. These revelations are a key to the greater reality, that's life itself, life abundance replete with love and happiness whereby challenges and difficulties become stepping stones.

In time you will realize that God gives you all you need. That it is God that guarantees all these things. That all you need is love. And it's love that makes you Godlike, and by being Godlike, you become spiritually self-sufficient. And it's this self-sufficiency that enables you to be what you should be, what you must be, what God designed you to be.

Such is a way to learn to progressively grow in our awareness as Soul, made in God's image, as we learn to stand on our own feet, thereby becoming masters of our own destiny. Keep in mind that there's wisdom in living a life guided by the inner voice of God. It's the voice of

God that knows more than your limited mind does. So it's wise to follow it. When you reach a stage where everything is guided from the inner, your entire life gets transformed. Everything you say and do becomes touched, to some degree, by the love of God.

Therein lies the key to living a life of Divine Spirit.

LOVING FOR THE GOOD OF ALL

You can start learning how to love for the good of all by letting love be the force that dictates all your actions. Let love be the force that guides your thinking. Let love be the force that inspires you to act. Let love be the force that teaches you about God. Let love be the force that counts above everything else. Learn to live by the law of love. Because love is the law of God that supersedes all other laws.

Once we learn to abide by the law of love, everything else falls into place. Thereafter, you will be drawn to places where you can share and receive more love as a necessary manifestation of love.

Like attracts like. Similarly, love attracts love. So all things love will be drawn to you equal to how much love you give. Give only in the spirit of Love so that you create an environment of love in which others come to share their love.

And that is the secret of loving for the good of all.

LIVING A LIFE FILLED WITH LOVE

What does it mean to live a life filled with love? What that means is that you go about your business with a loving attitude. A loving attitude steeped in the love for life and God, stemming from the discipline from living within laws of spirit. Meaning you listen to Divine spirit as much as it is practically possible while going on with your daily business as you align your actions with its dictates. In other words, spirit begins to direct your life in a way that benefits you immensely for it can only work consistent with its nature. Thus make your life more expansive and abundant. That's the benefit of aligning yourself with guidance from living a life infused with love. It is a life of high ethics born of following spirit's dictates. So that what's considered spiritually unethical should not be engaged in. Meaning anything that will retard one's spiritual growth should be avoided. And anything that advances your spiritual consciousness should be accepted with love for it further reenergizes you with love. This way you continue to make sure you are gradually growing in your capacity for more love.

A life lived with such unfailing obedience to inner guidance, and self-discipline is blessed with divine love.

A LIFE OF LOVE GUIDED BY THE WILL OF GOD

If you sincerely love God, you must give of yourself spiritually to serve God in your own way that fits your unique makeup. It is not the giving of yourself whereby you give up your material possessions, your interests, your job, and things of value to your life and become passive. But it is the giving up of your concerns, fears, and place your guidance and security into the hands of God. After this, you must learn to harmonize your will with that of Divine will. This means you bring under control your personal will so that there is harmony and alignment with God's will. When these are in place, you can't help but increasingly let Divine will operate through you. To a greater degree, the will of God will guide you to do things which before you may not have thought of. It will guide you to a richer and fuller life.

It is worthwhile to let your life be guided by the will of God. Listen for this inner guidance for God may speak anytime, any place, through someone else, a child, a beggar, a teacher, a coworker, your boss, or a stranger. Stay alert to that unknown presence of God, to that unexpected voice of God. It may come when you least expect it.

This inner voice of God comes by its own will, in its own time, and on its own terms. All you have to do is stay open to life's blessings. Stay open to life's happenings so you don't miss such opportunities when a message meant for you comes. Stay attuned to the rhythm of life for a better spiritual life, one guided by the will of God.

OBEDIENCE TO GOD

One way to express your love for God is by obeying God. You obey God by following through with *Its* edicts and aligning your actions accordingly.

These edicts are written in your heart. They are not written in the books written by man.

Because they hinge upon the personal relationship you establish with God. These commandments, in their true essence, in their higher form are customized to fit your unique individuality and your level of consciousness.

All governing laws have universal implications and personal ones. But there's always one law that overrides all laws. It is the law of love; it supersedes all other laws.

It is this love from which other laws stem. These inner personal commandments are written in the spirit of love. Love as it applies to your own individuality limited in its outer expression by your capacity and attitude.

Its outer form is shaped and expressed through our lim-ited human consciousness.

This pure love in its true spiritual nature is limitless and its source inexhaustible.

We can tap into this source via obedience to God.

LOVING GOD IN THE MOMENT

How do you love God in the moment? Realize that every minute spent in loving God is spent in eternity. Every minute invested in the discovery of truth, partaking of it, expressing it, sharing it, is a moment lived in eternity. To live in the loving arms of God, one must surrender to *It* on the daily basis. It's this surrender that opens your heart to the great mysteries of God. So it's essential to stay in the perpetual state of surrender to God. This way, you stay in harmony with God's truth. And the presence of God will be with you every day.

As you go about your daily life, try to realign and return to this moment. It is in living in the now that you become realigned with life. It is being in the moment that you reestablish the direct link with God. It is being present with God in the now that God becomes your daily companion.

So love God today, in this minute and your tomor-row will fall into place.

GOD NEEDS YOU

Does God really need us? if so in what way? God has endowed each one of us gifts and unique abilities which everyone has in their own way. They are what make you a unique Divine Spark of God. So God needs you as its distributing agent for its gifts that only you can in your own way. You carry a part of God that is very real and it is interwoven into God's fiber. So God needs you to give back to life God's gift imbedded in you. In giving it out, you receive more of it.

So give back to life what you have gained from life and God. Give back to life what God gave you. And that gift is the gift of love packaged according to each individual makeup, consciousness, and calling.

Love is the gift that manifests in your talents, abilities, skills, hobbies, interests, inclinations in a way that makes things better in your life and other people's lives. So your responsibility is to do what is humanly possible, with your best effort, with everything you have to improve life according to what you have spiritually. If you think you have nothing to give back it is because you have not recognized it.

If all you give back to life is your ego and its attendant boastful elements, you will fail spiritually sooner or later. So give only the good that is love, so life around you can be enriched and elevated.

That's what *God* asks of you in return for Its love for you—simply give back the best of you, the best of what are your gifts.

THE INVISIBLE HAND OF GOD

Each one of us is unique and different in our own individual makeup yet we come from the same source—God. Hence God needs you to identify and live up to your God given individual uniqueness. So let us work toward realizing the potential that lies within us. Each one of us is God's loving child in spite of yourself. So we need to realize that we are God's living truth. Our love for God should be the foundation of our life.

Once you realize God's ways and plans for you, you need to adjust your life and move toward a newly recognized spiritual life. A new life as dictated by God, your spiritual father, your inner guide, your creator. A life lived according to God's plan for you is a testament of God's presence in your daily life. A life that will inspire those around you, those with whom you come into contact, even those you may never ever meet in person but through your works, they will come to know God a little more.

Through you, an invisible hand of God may touch others and inspire them to rise to higher heights, and inspire them to do great things. So stay open and obedient to Its guidance for God needs you for who you are - as a gift to the world.

YOUR DAILY GUIDE

Who better to be your daily guide than God? It's either you follow God or you follow the negative force. These are the only two options. But how do you know you are following God? Listen to your heart and the answer will be revealed to you. First, start by surrendering all you do to God, letting go of your fixed outmoded ways to eliminate or minimize any interference with new guidance which may come your way.

What does that mean and entail? Letting go of your actions, thoughts, concerns, fears, trusting your instincts, and trusting God that all will work out. God works through your feelings to steer you to love, to prompt you, and guide your thinking to act in a certain way that is aligned with God's way. So listen to your feelings, gut feeling, which in that state of surrender influences and gives rise to the right thought processes and right attitude. When this happens, you are allowing God to be your guide on a daily basis, in all things you do, in things you feel, and in things you think, big and small alike. This does not mean you will always be aware that God is working through you nor does it mean you won't make mistakes in life. Mistakes serve a purpose. They are an indication that we are growing as long as we are learning from them and not keep repeating the same mistakes over and over again.

GOD'S ACTIONS THROUGH YOU

In order for you to become better channels for God, you can start by rearranging your life, within your power, get rid of things of no real value that negatively impact your life. Strive to minimize creating negative karma by making better choices. Depending on the choices you make, you can either cause adverse conditions for which you would unnecessarily suffer or create favorable conditions, making your life a joy to live. So, take action where you need to. But don't let your actions be dictated by fear. In order to stay open to the hand of God, use love as your guiding principle. With love you can spiritually conquer anything. It helps to remember that with a loving attitude, you can open others' hearts. And with an open heart, God can work through you. Armed with God's light, you can bring light to others. And their walls of illusion and resistance they built up through ignorance will begin to break down. Nothing can serve them, save God, if they let It.

One way you can reach others is through humility. So learn to humble yourself before God so you may act as one of its clear channels. Through you as its clear channel, God will work with you under all conditions no matter how fixed they may appear. So let God work through you in your efforts to resolve any trouble spots in your daily life and those you meet where warranted.

The hand of God supersedes all other lower corruptible man's hands. It is helpful to allow the hand of *God* to yield maximum positive results. Learn to step back to let the hand of God guide us in the direction in accord with Divine will.

LIFE OF LOVE

LOVE AND TRUTH

When you put love in everything you do, love comes back to you a hundredfold. Love, the only element that will sustain us without diminishing if given from the heart.

In love there is truth. And in truth lies strength. *Strength* becomes the backbone upon which love grows. Love and truth in our actions and speech build character. Things gravitate toward one who has love and truth in their heart.

Untruth diminishes the quality of love and compromises one's character. Whereas Love has the power to open one's heart to greater truth, it is the path of truth that leads one to self-discovery. Discovery of Soul self clarifies one's spiritual needs. With that, one's mission becomes clear at a deeper level. With this new clarity, things of little or no value fall away. And things that are spiritually beneficial to you come into your world for your benefit. Such is the power of love. Because with love, you have everything you need spiritually.

LOVE BECOMES YOU AS YOU BECOME LOVE

Love is you as you are love in that you as Soul, are made from the loving cloth of God. When you realize what lies behind love, when you understand what love is, when you know the inner workings of love, when you awaken to the reality of love, when you know what love can do, when you understand the essence of love, when you see love in all things, when you see all actions as love, when you embrace love in its fullness, when you do all actions with love, when you come to the realization that nothing else matters but love, that its love only that can take you from where you are now to the next level, you come to realize that it is love only that can open your heart for God to make its presence known. An open heart opens the door to the presence of God.

To love with an open heart is to embrace and attract life in its fullness. To love with this open heart is the key to serving life selflessly. When you serve life from the place of love within, you are becoming love as love becomes you.

CLIMBING TO GREATER SPIRITUAL HEIGHTS

When you have love, it propels you to greater spiritual heights, beyond reach of human consciousness. Because love is the only building block that has power to catapult us to Godhood. Love nourishes what you start and follow through. Love lends strength and sustains what you set out to achieve if you stay focused. Go for love, and the entire world will move with you if not follow you. For love uplifts and the world tends toward moving up and forward.

The power of love is the greatest power ever if coupled with courage. Greatness is a mark of truth, power, and courage to do what seems humanly impossible. This takes implicit faith in the magical power of love. Love without faith and trust will sooner or later make your efforts falter and what you set out to accomplish may not come to full fruition.

Faith opens the flow of the power of love. Unshakeable belief in the power of love can create a pathway for love to come through to help you climb the heights to greatness.

Because it is only primarily the power of love that can move you to do great things. Not great in an egotistical way, but in a humble way and for the greater good.

In love alone lies the latent power of greatness. Unleash it, partake of it, live it, and you'll make this world a better place for self and others.

SERVING LIFE

There are as many ways to serve life as there are people. God has instilled in each one of us a gift suited to our individual makeup. When *God* gives us a gift of any kind, we must cultivate it and make use of it to serve life. To serve life with grace and love.

Instead, we often allow the ego self to take over and fall into a trap of serving our ego self.

When *God* gives us a gift of any kind and we misapply it, we do ourselves a disfavor and often the full gift can never fully be realized in the environment of self-service. If we use it to impress others, we sidetrack into the negative path. We squander the spiritual power.

The spiritual power never intends to show off. It does not do things with funfare. It's too humble to parade its achievements and miracles. And it should rightly be so for it's under conditions of humility that God's spirit finds fertile grounds to plant its seeds. Seeds that sooner or later manifest as opportunities for serving life even more.

If we allow God's power to freely work through us, we would accomplish great works never before imagined.

Because God's power knows no limits. It's not bound by human laws. So to serve life effectively, one needs to humble oneself before God and ask with sincerity the best way to serve life with gifts one has. This will guide one to the right contacts, places, situations, where one can serve with love in the best way possible. All one needs to do is to ask honestly and the answer shall come in some way, sooner or later. And when the answer is received, and it feels spiritually right, by God, do all you can to make this a reality. Put your heart into it. Keep in mind that you are doing this not for self, but for the greater good. That the only sure way to serve life truly is by giving of ourselves fully to the cause on which we have embarked.

Be careful how you serve. Serve life with love. Do not clamor for recognition.

It is only when something is done to gain others recognition that we fall into a negative trap. To serve life truly, fully to the best of our ability, we need to be the best we can be and do the best in the name of God without expectation of praise.

LIVING LIFE FULLY

Life is how we view it. With time and right spiritual training, our universe should expand beyond the limited outer existence. To an existence far beyond the stars and moons of this earth world.

As our inner vision opens, doors of other worlds begin to open up to new possibilities of life experience beyond. We begin to awaken to the reality that Life does not end or begin here. It is exhilarating to learn that life goes on beyond the portals of death. Life becomes ever more complex and of great an adventure as our vision expands to universes that remain invisible to an untrained eye. Universes that are bigger, richer, more bountiful, where finite becomes infinite, where the ugly becomes all consuming beautiful, where darkness becomes light, where assumption does not exist, where pretense is not allowed entry. Where life is lived for what it is in the truest of spiritual sense. This is life lived in fullness, in spirit, in *God* here and beyond.

BLESSINGS FROM DIVINE SPIRIT

We all receive blessings from divine spirit in one way or another that befits us. Sometimes they come even without our asking for them. The blessings may come even when we are not thinking about them. Divine Spirit has its own innate infinite foresight and intelligence to determine when and where the blessings are needed. But often they come when we need them most. But we may not realize in our limited consciousness that it was what we needed to ask for. Divine spirit may intervene and pour out its gifts.

Soul, divine spirit, *God* that operates by higher laws always knows the right answer even before a question is raised in our human consciousness. If we ask the right question, the answer would be hinted at within the question. So, how we frame the questions may determine how we get the answers.

With an open heart, allowing and letting the Divine Spirit flow without directing *It*, the gift would come through our stream of consciousness at the right time. We would recognize it without questions, qualms or hesitation. With deeper insight, mind uncluttered by doubts, fears, anxieties, we would gain an in-depth knowingness beyond doubt, beyond the limits of our minds what blessings are coming to us. With that, our lives would become a little more forgiving. This is the power of the gift of insight into life's blessings that make life easier and more enjoyable each day.

LIVING A DETACHED LIFE

In our pursuit to do the right thing, often we wind up doing a wrong thing. In our pursuit to live a life guided by divine spirit, often we wind up living a life guided by our egos. In our pursuit to make right decisions, often we make decisions misguided by our fears, anxieties, passions of our minds. In our efforts to follow Soul's direction, often we end up following dictates of the mind. In our pursuit to seek guidance from *God*, often we find guidance from our mind. Everything seems to lead to the mind. We are unwittingly too dependent on the mind for all the answers and guidance.

All we need is simply let go of our hold on our thoughts, opinions, and fears.

In that state of inner detachment, we will learn the power of living a life of freedom from the control of our minds.

A detached life is a life lived in freedom from the shackles of this world. Freedom to stand on our own feet with complete reliance on Divine Spirit for guidance and protection yet remain fully engaged in our daily life.

WHAT IS SURRENDER?

When we let go of our strong attachments to our negative thoughts, strong opinions, mental questioning, and mental gymnastics, we allow spirit to take over. We are saying to Divine spirit "we can't handle this at a personal level". We are asking *God* to guide us toward the right avenue. We are asking *God* to steer us in the right direction. *God* can see beyond what the human eye can see. *God* can change circumstances beyond our control. *God* knows what is good for us.´ *God* knows our life cycles, our right partner, our right job, our right diet, It will bring into our being and our reach all things at the right time that are beneficial to us. The challenge is how to figure out and recognize when the guidance to what we need comes.

One thing we can do is watch for the signs, clues about what is going on around us and within us, surrender to God our cares, fears, limitations, and in turn, we get what we need in right proportion at the right time on God's terms.

LOVE FROM UNEXPECTED PLACES

Love is universal, yet it is personal, for it is channeled through you as its operating distributor. To be a good love distributer, one ought to learn its ways, its inner workings, its philosophy, its power, its reality. How it manifests at human level vs. global level.

If you keep your heart open, love will show you its ways and how to give it and when to give it and how much of it to give out.

In love is truth at its core. Fear implies presence of untruth. Therefore a search for truth is in effect a search for love. Love and truth coexist to enhance and build on each other. So that when you love truth, this in turn yields greater capacity for love.

Its manifestation will vary depending on the situation and the needs at hand. At times it will come to you directly but other times disguised if the moment calls for that. At times under the guise of something else so as to slip through a conditioned mind which expects love to come in a certain specific predetermined way. To the extent that the mind likes routine and familiarity, it can be a barrier to love when it comes in a way unfamiliar to it. You bypass this by keeping an open heart for the unexpected for love can sometimes come from unexpected places in unexpected ways.

DIFFERENT MANIFESTATIONS OF LOVE

Love comes in different forms, so it helps to learn to recognize them.

Kindness is a form of love. It's love that is expressed through acts done out of consideration of another person in need.

Patience is a form of love. When you are patient, you can render service to life more in tune with the natural rhythm of life. When you love life, you will take time to learn lessons of love embedded in a given situation which could otherwise be lost by rushing. If you rush, you will stumble, and fall and life's lessons of love therein lost.

Courage is a form of love. Courage is a form of ability to render service where and when needed irrespective of how daunting and scary the situation may be.

Truth and courage go hand in hand for love to be expressed to the optimum level. Truth implies an absence of fear and a presence of love. Thus truth in essence is love. If untruth unites with courage, the result is brutality in ones actions. With sincerity, patience, love for truth, kindness, supported by courage, you can learn to recognize love in its many different forms. This will render you spiritually richer than ever before.

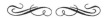

TALK LOVE TODAY

To infuse love in what you say, try this simple exercise; firstly fill your heart with love. Use this as a backdrop from which you try to speak. Then talk with love to others even though you don't mention the word love.

Love must be behind every word you say. It must be behind every word that drops out of your mouth. So, remember that every speech, every word must be driven with the force of love. If you do this, you will make a *connection* with the people you meet. They will remember your uplifting words as driven by love at a conscious or unconscious level.

So, talk love today, tomorrow, every day. For in it lies the secret of love in action expressed through speech.

LOVE: THE KEY TO ALL LIFE

Without love, you have nothing. So, surrender yourself to love. In surrendering, you will experience love in a profound way. It behooves you to embrace it and live it greatly. In doing so, it will bring out your own unique individuality in you as no two people are ever alike. It's this uniqueness that touches people that will set you apart from others. That's what happens when you come from a place of love in what you say, what you do, what you think.

Everything will work well even though at times they may seem to be going awry to the human eye.

Miracles will begin to happen because in giving out love from the core of your heart, you touch the core of God in you. And it's that which begins to influence and run your life. Your life becomes more dynamic, because Divine Spirit is actively engaged and expressed in your life through loving actions. It moves your life forward if you are willing to move along with it. It makes your life abundant if you let it guide you and you align your actions with its impeccable guidance.

All you need is a dose of courage, patience, plan, and action. And your life will never be the same seemingly random, dreary, mundane journey.

GIVING BACK TO LIFE

When you give something without expecting anything in return, you allow God to determine the course of its effects. But when you give something and expect something back, you are imposing human limitations in it. This limits how far our actions can affect what we do, the nature and character of the effect. So if you want to have maximum spiritual effect on your actions, step back and let God be in charge of the effect of your actions. This kind of attitude yields not only greater love and trust for God but also a stronger bond between you and God.

In giving back to life without expecting anything in return, you are giving a gift that keeps on giving. A gift that enriches the recipient in more ways more than one. In ways in which an invisible connection of unity gets established between the sender and receiver. This makes for a better relationship with those we love and serve.

YOU CAN HAVE YOUR LIFE IN ORDER AGAIN

One way to start to put your life in order again can be by introduction of God into your life. You can start by learning to love God as though there's nothing else that matters in the world. In principle, nothing should matter save God, if you want to seek the highest within you. When you are filled with God's love, it's love that opens your heart to all possibilities. Possibilities that are provided for you by Divine Spirit. So if you love God truly, God will grant you these possibilities. Divine Spirit operates in such a way that it moves life forward. It is dynamic and responsive to our individual needs that are in keeping with its nature. Thus It will guide one once engaged in whatever you do that is in alignment with its nature.

Understand this basic principle so your life can be put in order again. And yes you can have your life reordered by Divine Spirit. All you need to do is simply surrender to Its impeccable guidance. And It will elevate you to highest heights. For it is in seeking the highest that the rest of our life falls into place.

GETTING OUT OF TROUBLE

With love, things reorganize themselves to a new order to allow more love to flow. That's why the way of love is the way to heaven on earth. Heaven on earth predicated on the state of consciousness you carry. We are the ones who determine our heaven by our inner state.

Trouble out here means trouble on the inner side of things within us. To start to resolve troubles in our lives we don't have to look further than our inner state. Spiritual solutions are always within us. And God within is the key to the answer. And love we allow is the catalyst to the resolution of problems. So listen to God and follow the path of love. That's an important guiding principle to live by. If you live by this principle, your life will be redirected in the right way. You will awaken to miracles and greater awareness of the ever loving presence of God in your life. You will begin to see possibilities where before were impossibilities. You'll see solutions where before existed none. You will overcome obstacles, where before you gave up out of fear and feeling of inadequacy. Because the power of love can overcome anything, it is the highest power there is and will ever be.

SERVING LIFE WITH LOVE

Every action you do selflessly and with love serves life. Every action you do should be imbued with love. How do you do that? Place your attention on God. This changes the quality of the action. In so doing, you are permitting God to work with you. God uses love as a tool to serve life. So that when you serve life with love, Divine Sprit is serving life through you.

So serve life with love by keeping your attention on God. This spiritualizes your inner consciousness. And all you touch and do with love will turn to gold. It is a discipline worth cultivating.

APPRECIATING GOD MORE

How do you appreciate God more? Learn to take a step back and look at life events closely and watch the play of spirit. The recognition of spirit at work is a function of an honest and steadfast engagement of your spiritual faculties of sight and hearing. The more you use them, the more acute your spiritual senses become. The increased clarity enables you to see God's actions more clearly, even the minutest of details if needed.

Once you embrace God with your whole being, you have embarked truly on the road home to God. You will appreciate the miracle of God's creations because you can now see more a common thread of God essence that runs through all life.

It's your increased awareness of *It* that makes you appreciate and love God more.

SHARING LOVE

True love does not seek to dominate. Love in its true expression should not hurt when it is given and expressed sincerely and correctly. In other words, consideration and listening to one's heart is key in giving love when and where needed. Otherwise, the gift of love would be wasted or create unexpected undesired results. One may end up unwittingly taking advantage of another or make the mistake of taking love for granted. This simply means that one ought to be thoughtful, careful, alert, aware, and wise in sharing love. In order to share love with others, we need to remember how to correctly do it. Love should be the mainstay for all your actions.

Giving love to others is a skill you develop. You learn when to give it at the right time. Many times such opportunities are missed because they catch us off guard. In other instances they may seem impossible so we pass them. Yet it's such chances that afford us the opportunity to grow beyond where we are.

So step up to the plate and seize the opportunity to share love whenever it presents itself, when able.

HOW CAN I SERVE GOD MORE?

You serve God by doing things that God guides you to do. God has a dream for each one of us. By fulfilling God's dreams for you, you serve God more. You serve God more by committing yourself to Its mission for you. You serve God more by allowing yourself to be *Its* servant.

Being *Its* servant implies being a servant to life, thus serving others. So once you know what God is asking you to do, and you do it despite what the world may say in opposition, you are truly serving God more. You could serve God more by recognizing God's gifts for you, accepting them, and partaking of them. This will enrich your life beyond your wildest dreams. And this will put you in a better position to serve God more.

The more you receive from God, the more you have to give back to life. Thus the more you in turn serve God more.

EVERYTHING CHANGES
WITH LOVE

When things change, it is not necessarily because life has bestowed them upon you—but surely born out of your actions. Actions done with love will bring about positive changes. But be careful, sometimes positive changes are preceded by chaos. Chaos arising from the breaking down of old patterns of negative conditions. But it takes patience and strength not to panic and lose one's bearings in the middle of apparent chaos. Because once you lose yourself in the apparent confusion, often temporary, you may make wrong choices that may lead you in a wrong direction.

So there's great wisdom in taking one's time to learn well lessons imbedded in the apparent confusion or chaos. For with patience, the dust will eventually settle, rendering things clearer. In the moment of clarity, you will regain your footing and enjoy the good fruits born of change.

Now ready to move on further with newly gained wisdom, expanded capacity for love, greater joy, increased spiritual strength, because with love all these things are possible. One of the things you can do is learn to be patient, never force issues and let things unfold naturally.

WHEN TRUE LOVE ENTERS ONE'S LIFE

How can you create conditions to let true love enter your life? Among other ways, there are spiritual exercises that can help begin to expand one's consciousness such as the HU song. With expanded consciousness comes increased capacity for love. Expansion of consciousness begins on the inner and this impacts your outer consciousness in the like manner. Inner growth leads to outer changes but we have to match our actions with our inner growth. This makes for a balanced integrated ever evolving individual.

One feature about expanded consciousness is that it speeds up one's pace in life because one can now live a life of greater responsibility and can handle more on account of newly attained spiritual strength. Your circle of experience expands in proportion to the degree that your inner world has grown as you make corresponding adjustments in the outer. While before, you may only have had a few friends, interests, experiences and choices, now because of your expanded consciousness, you gain greater freedom, strength, wisdom and love. Your world becomes bigger, richer, and more dynamic. Your love for life increases in strength and depth. Your interests become anew and deeper. Your values become highly refined and more ethical.

Because everything changes for the better when pure love enters one's life, you will no longer be the little old self, you will wake up to your true self as Soul, a spark of God!

A LIFE OF ACTION

When your life is guided by love, miracles follow. Love ensures that there is continual outflow of Divine Spirit in your life as a daily practical reality. Life may become filled with joy, love, adventure, and beauty. These elements coexist to confirm the salubrious impact of the power of the presence of God. Your life and that of the presence of Divine Spirit become inseparable. This infuses your life with vibrancy and increased liveliness. That's the key to life of action driven by love.

It's a life of surrender to that which is greater than human Self. A life of enjoyment yet lived in moderation. A life that is spiritually charged that lends itself to continual growth. A life filled with action, adventure and lived in obedience to God's will. Living in obedience to God's will, one cannot fail. Because the active presence of God engenders expansion of one's life. And to ensure this remains so, one must live from the heart and unfailingly lean upon the support of the infallible Divine Spirit. With love like this, life becomes worth living.

LOVE IS A JOURNEY

How is love a journey? When you love from the core of your heart, unconditoinally, you begin to move toward the source of love - God, the eternal. To love is to live in eternity. To live in eternity now, one must love truthfully and wisely. Because where there is love, there is truth. Truth in thought and action determines the quality of the moment. Higher truth is characterized by the higher quality of the eternal moment within the confines of the consciousness to which it pertains. To live in eternity is to always live in the moment of truth and to aspire to the highest truth within one. And the journey one must travel must begin within one. And the truth one must discover lies within one. Within this discovery, one finds out one's inner splendor, one's inner higher true self, that indeed one is above all labels society attributes to him, but a higher being that belongs not here, but to the higher pure world of God governed by the overriding law of love.

With this discovery, one can embrace life, fully knowing that the journey home to God starts and ends within one.

HOW DO YOU LIVE IN ACCORD WITH GOD'S WILL?

While it is essential to be self sufficient as part of our fulfillment of the cosmic plan, also remember that your life is not for you alone. It's supposed to be lived for the greater good. And in turn it will benefit you more. So when you live life to make life better for others, your life gets better in the process. When you live your life such that only you benefit from it, doing others little good, it becomes a selfish life done for self-indulgence. Such a life is a selfish one, truly a life out of synch with God's law of love.

There is spiritual wisdom in living a life of self-abnegation, lived in moderation, sacrifice for the greater good, and a life of self discipline. This requires one to surrender to God's will. A life lived in such state of constant selflessness is a life of Godliness. And it's in living such a life that we fulfill God's dream for us. Only then do we become as God designed us to be.

God needs you as much you need *It* because you are an integral part of its spiritual makeup. Thus God needs your life much more than you realize. Hence God expects you to live your life in accord with Its will and Its loving guidance.

MOVING ON

Love has the power to open doors to all opportunities that afford one a chance to grow spiritually. Doors that lead to greater opportunities for self-advancement. Doors that take you from smaller rooms to bigger rooms. Doors that can never be opened by any other key save Love as the password that unlocks the doors.

Life therefore can be viewed as comprising of innumerable rooms, each one with its own experiences designed to strengthen us spiritually. These experiences gradually yield wisdom, freedom, and higher love. There is no end to growing in our capacity for more love. There is always another key to be earned for entry into another room, always a larger room. And each successive larger room comes with it its own gifts, obstacles, lessons, all designed to make us stronger and better. It's up to us to walk through the door to get all the gifts we need that pertain to that room during that time period.

If we fulfill the conditions needed to move on to the next room—the larger room, we will have grown measurably in our capacity for more love. With more love so gained, we are ready to move on to new experiences as we journey on home to God.

MESSENGERS OF LOVE

When you love life, when you love others, when you love everything around you, when you have love for your fellowman, and when you can give goodwill to others from your heart, you will have a good relationship with life. When you can be sincere in your heart and give of yourself and wish all well, when you can feel this truly in your heart, when you can wish success to your competitors, when you can honestly wish all well with purity of thought, you can rest assured your heart will open up to the music of God. You can rest assured your heart will pulsate to the universal rhythm of life. You can rest assured you'll wake up to the secret truth around you and within you. You can rest assured you will be one of the few spiritually alive among the dead.

Those who are attuned to the needs of others often are a blessing and a light to those in need. They become messengers of love who enliven not only their lives but also those they serve.

LOVING OTHERS

The value of love lies not in its abstraction but truly in your actions. Watch how you give of yourself to others, putting yourself in their shoes to better understand their needs. This will change how you relate to them and how you serve them. Be careful with what secret thoughts you hold in your mind. Keep your thoughts clean for they may manifest in your outer reality.

Watch how you work; your work ethic will say a lot about the quality of your character. Sacrifice for others when the occasion calls for it for the good of another.

All these are aspects of love expressed in the human state. It helps to remember that love should not be locked within your human consciousness. You must manifest it, pass it on.

For it to be of any value, you must demonstrate it to those you love. It would help if you made it a reality for it to be of any practical value to you and those you serve.

Actions driven by love activate the dormant love lying within the depth of our hearts.

Once activated, share it, give it out where needed. Be practical and commonsensical about it to make it a daily active and helpful part of you. It's by doing daily selfless deeds for which you expect no repayment that you truly live this love.

So go out in the world, be observant, be alert, be ready, be willing, be proactive, love others selflessly, serve life for that's your underlying mission on earth.

LOVE'S WAY

Love touches us in many ways, some of which are as follows: It enables us to reconnect with God via the Divine Spirit, it enables us to find our right religion or spiritual path or spiritual master, it opens hearts which otherwise would be closed including ours, and it enables us to connect with others at a profound level.

Find love, be love, have love, give love, share love, think love, breathe love. And love will become you as you become love. The best way to love is to give up the little Self. The little Self cannot comprehend the full concept of love, so it fights it.

Once the little self is brought under control, the higher Self that operates under a different and higher law takes over. This enables love to begin to pour out to the appropriate open ready and willing recipients around you, near and far, invisible and visible.

Just be careful how you give it. Don't take credit for dividends that come your way.

They are love's way of rewarding your selfless acts of love.

DOING THINGS IN GOD'S NAME

It is helpful to learn to let God be the basis of all your actions. Without God, you are on your own. Yet God is always with you through your inner channels, sometimes with the help of inner spiritual guides sometimes referred to as Angels. God works through many religions or spiritual paths depending on which one fits you, each with its respective spiritual leader, savior, or guru, in most cases who are no longer living here in the physical plane. For instance in ECKANKAR, the path of spiritual freedom, its spiritual leader Harold Klemp, the Mahanta, the Living ECK Master, helps students toward attainment of spiritual freedom. Each person should look within their inner temple and follow their right path that speaks to their heart. And none can determine and decide what path to follow, save yourself. So follow your inner spiritual guidance in search of God, do all in God's name, and you will be led to truth. Because in truth lies God's power.

It behooves you to open yourself to allow your actions to be touched by God's hand.

So do everything with the belief and knowledge that God's love is in action, in your thoughts, and feelings as much as practically possible. Have no concern for any negativity but recognize it for what it is and deal with it accordingly for in it are lessons of love. So look at apparent negativity as blessings in disguise. Stay focused on doing all in God's name and your life will run a little easier though not necessarily easy.

THE KEY TO SPIRITUALITY

Love is the key to spirituality because it opens your heart to God. With an open heart, the spirit of God can enter your heart and make its residence there. It becomes your guest. A guest that serves you as you in turn serve *It*. With this interchange between yourself and God, you become one with the light of God. You become one with the Sound of God. You become one with the Divine Spirit. And the Divine Spirit in a sense becomes you.

You become a living, pulsating and a spiritually charged individual. Different from when you didn't allow love to be an active and conscious part of your daily life. This spiritual realization through love attained by drenching yourself with love, becoming love itself, becoming an active part itself, becoming love intoxicated and finally becoming God-intoxicated, is the key to spirituality. And you sustain it by keeping an open heart.

WORKING WITH GOD ON A DAILY BASIS

Working with God on a daily basis means consulting with God in all of one's affairs, actions, plans, and decisions as much as is practically possible, and it does not mean you become irresponsible. Do what you have to do with what you have and turn to God to help you where and when needed. When you work with God, you are in effect saying to God, guide me, show me your way, show me how to make you a reality in my life. When you come to God, you are permitting God to work with you, to be allowed as a conscious part of your daily life. God will show you how to live life better in a spiritually correct way, rendering your life more meaningful and vibrant. This means a life lived in a more conscious spiritual state - recognizing what a miracle this life is.

Strive to always look God to avoid as well as enable you to overcome unnecessary traps, uncalled for inconveniences that often come through our ignorance and stubbornness. God, if allowed to work through you, it will bring wonders into your life. You need to just learn to trust it, give of yourself to *It*, and align your actions with the guidance you receive that you believe and understand from God. By so doing, you are aligning your will with God's will. And this is what it takes to work with God on a daily basis.

BECOMING A MORE REALIZED SPARK OF GOD

You must realize that without love as an active part of your life, you have nothing. You exist because God made it so. You love because God enabled you to for your spiritual sustenance and nourishment.

You laugh because God set it up that you are able to express joy through laughter. You smile because God knew that you would express its unseen loving presence through your smile for it expresses the happy nature of Soul within you hiding behind the façade of one's mask of social consciousness.

You are God in essence because *It* has instilled in you Its elements, Its Spirit.

So that what you become is more in the likeness of the Spirit It has placed in you. To express your love for God, it is best done by the way you conduct yourself in your daily life. Remember to give back to life that which you have gained from God as gifts to be passed on to the world. This is what you do as you become a realized Divine spark of God.

LIVING LIFE TO ITS FULLEST

Life must be lived and not wasted. How then do you live life fully? By being an active part of it. You do so by immersing yourself in it. How do you do that? By letting Divine Spirit guide you in all you do. As you go on living your daily life, place your trust and heart in God. When you place your trust in God, you will rise beyond your self imposed limitations. Divine Spirit will go ahead of you to prepare the way. You will begin to see miracles happening around you because you allow God to take charge of your affairs.

Since God is the creator, It has the power to recreate your life if you let It. To let It you must submit and surrender to It. It is surrender that opens the human gate to allow the reentry of Divine Spirit. To maintain this state of conscious union with spirit, surrender is key for it yields a deeper connection with divine Spirit. And it is in this that you live your life fully.

LEARNING HOW TO SURVIVE

Love for what you do is a key element in becoming successful in anything of worth. Because if you don't have love for what you are setting out to accomplish, you are liable to endure unnecessary stress and constraints. If you love something and you put out necessary effort, it will more likely work for you. Only you have to fulfill conditions for it to work.

You can start by setting out goals that are attainable in a spiritual and physical sense.

This helps focus the energy so it is not dispersed in all sorts of directions. Once goals are identified and established, move to achieve them. Though these goals may be mundane in outlook, they must be rooted in the desire directed toward spiritual quest for Soul to become more aware of its own nature and its spiritual potentiality. You learn to grow in awareness at each stage of each goal attained. Soul, in the process, learns how to survive on earth progressively in dimension and self-awareness. This leads, step by step, toward increased awareness of who you are as Indestructible Soul.

You gain freedom to soar above the entrapments of this world. You, as Soul, have now gained wisdom on what it takes to survive here on earth.

If you can't make it here, how do you expect to make it in the higher inner worlds commonly called heaven?

So start here and become a success here before you can expect to succeed in the world beyond.

HELP FROM DIVINE SPIRIT

Living life, in part, means experiencing pains and joys that come with it. If you are not feeling well, it helps to remember that it is part of the growth process. Some days you feel great. Other days you don't feel so great. The days you don't feel great are days you need to stop to examine your life to find out what's not working and why. Is it your attitude? Could it be a Divine law you violated knowingly or unknowingly?

Is it your actions? Is it your thoughts? Could it be something you did in the past coming back for remedial reason so as to restore balance, settle the score? Once you recognize that you may have in some way played a role, you should not give excuses for things not working. Once you accept responsibility, with such recognition, things will begin to unravel.

Often, conditions we find ourselves in are our own creations. We can, to some extent, control our attitude towards them henceforth. We can limit the unfavorable conditions once they become manifest and getting out of hand and counteract them instead of reacting negatively toward them.

Recognize what needs to be done and proceed from there. An illness maybe caused by a myriad of things, even such as our interference in another person's cycle. Once we recognize our violation, we let go of that action and attitude and just bless the negative condition. Sooner or later that negative energy will dissipate.

Recant the wrong tightly long held outmoded views, hand over into the hands of Divine Spirit, and say, "Thy will be done." Help will follow on God's own terms, in its own time, and in its own way.

GIVING LOVE TO OTHERS

Giving Love to others is not always as easy as it sounds. One can easily fall into the trap of being a people pleaser and mistake it for love. Love is universal; therefore, it comes in different ways and forms relative to each individual situation. Loving another could be as simple as showing respect to another person. It is not limited to just people and animals, It could also be love for truth, a hobby, an interest, a job, anything. It can also come in our conduct, such as being firm to instill discipline. Hence, being firm, does not always come from a position of power, but sometimes truly from love. It can also be gentle too, when there is easy flow of mutual trust, understanding and respect.

Give love to others not because they deserve it, but because it is the law of God that Soul needs to abide by for its survival and nourishment. How you give it is important.

Give it incorrectly, and you create unintended opposite effects. Give it correctly, and you open someone's heart. So be wary of how you give it.

Many give love with conditions; therefore, expect something in return for the favor or in their minds: It's a waste. They don't realize that the return gift may come in another form they may not associate with the love they gave another. So they blindly impose conditions inadvertently limit the love they are sharing. If you can't give love without conditions then don't give at all. It doesn't do anyone any good in the long run. It leads to enslavement of the recipient and the benefactor too.

If we were to give without expecting anything in return, life would reward us a hundredfold. If we were to give without placing conditions on the person we are giving, life would repay us either through the person we gave the gift or through another way unrecognizable by our limited human mind. Life always gives back in some way, if not sooner then later. That's why a person who always gives where and when needed and when able, always receives blessings from life in some way.

For in giving love there is a power beyond measure.

LOVE AND RELATIONSHIPS

In the human state, we can't love everyone equally. We are not built that way. We live in a world of limitations. Thus even in how we give love, there will be inbuilt limitations from a practical standpoint. It would be foolish to think you can love everyone the same. How someone affects you and vice versa how you affect the other person will determine the type of love and relationship you may have with that person.

If someone evokes ill feelings in you in their presence and by the thought of them, be careful, this may be a recipe for a bad relationship. We sometimes respond to people's private thoughts and secret intentions that are not often visibly obvious at human level.

In the human state, we often put on a mask and hide our ulterior motives, if we have them. To one with an honest and awakened heart, these covert intentions can be laid bare. In choosing whom to love, we can apply the principle of listening to our heart. Watch your feelings, listen to your heart, then your mind after. Then watch the outer for the connection of the dots. If you are humble enough, spirit will show you or confirm for you in someway, leaving no doubt in your mind about a particular aspect of truth or insight.

Giving love involves action on your part in some way. Either being available for someone in need of our attention, helping out in coin, and many number of ways materially or time-wise. Use common sense regarding whom to love or choose for a mate.

One needs to look at a lot of factors. Having many common grounds implies having fewer areas of disagreement and this could translate into a more harmonious relationship.

Common goals and interests cannot be emphasized enough. They are unifying points in a relationship. The more you have, the better, the stronger, the happier, the longer-lasting and more fulfilling your relationship will be. Without these common points of interest you are left with a relationship with divergent interests; thus, a lot of areas in which there may be less reason to support and appreciate the value of another. One will tend not to value the other out of the perceived notion that what one is involved in is of little or no value, automatically leading one to be judgmental. That already becomes recipe for discontent in a relationship. Two people will sooner or later grow apart. The magic power of love soon dies.

The end of a relationship becomes an inevitability, sooner or later.

So, follow your heart, stay sincere, be alert, it's rewarding beyond words to find someone with whom to share love.

BE THE BEST THAT YOU CAN EVER BE

Go to work and be the best that you can ever be. Maintain your professionalism to the best of your ability. Do what needs to be done efficiently and effectively. To make God present in your life, you must do your best and aspire to excellence. Once this is done, you'll touch God's essence and those around you may feel it. They will like being in your presence because verily they are in the presence of Divine Spirit that is alive in you.

So be the best that you can ever be. It's God's way of making Itself present in your life. Through your actions, it will manifest itself. IT manifests Itself through actions of high standards and done with love. Such actions bring about a feeling of love, awe and wonder. This is so because it is indeed God in action through you. Through your dedication and love of what you do.

So be the best you can ever be, and the presence of God will be your reward.

PURE LOVE

When pure loves dawns, thoughts of the beloved evoke a warm feeling of love and elation. What is it that causes a subtle elation about the person? Is it an anticipation of something good to happen? Once you have this experience, you want to recapture it again and again. It's never a selfish emotion. It's never a love that is imposing. It's the type that makes one feel serene within one's inner being. It is a feeling that transcends sappy emotions. There is purity to its quality. It's a feeling with no boundaries in its effect.

Thinking about one can evoke feelings of warmth yet it transcends thought. Thought has the power to bring the beloved into closer proximity. Because spirit being, as we are, are not limited by space and time. Such that the time we think about a person we, by unbounded divine nature of divine spirit, come into our presence. Thus a feeling of warmth ensues.

So when we think about some people, and feel at ease with them it is because we are in harmony with them. If we feel at odds with them, a feeling of discord permeates us, it could be a red flag, be careful about such a one. People's private ill intentioned thoughts have a way of reaching us through our feelings before these thoughts come into visible manifestation. Such feelings of disharmony could portend danger to our wellbeing.

Some people could usurp our kindness and try to take advantage of it. Some are channels of the negative force knowingly or unknowingly. With such people, this sense of disharmony becomes more apparent with their proximity. Because by proximity, forces interface thus cause increased awareness of imminent clash within physical striking distance. Sometimes it helps not to be around people like this because inwardly they maybe hypercritical of us, in turn we become self critical, they put us on the defense, turning our attention in on ourselves, thus boxing us inside ourselves. This can lead to closure of our hearts, with that, we shrink in our spiritual stature and well being. Consequently, our sense of well spiritual being becomes undermined. So be wise, be selective in whom you choose for a trusting friend. They could be an enemy, an agent of the dark force in disguise, out to destroy your dreams.

Where there's pure, innocent, trusting love, between two people, magic happens.

If there is great harmony and attraction between two people, physical proximity will heighten a sense of physical desire for each other with an urge to express it. Soon the inevitable may occur. Pure love does not hurt the other.

It uplifts, it purifies, it warms the heart of the lover and the beloved alike.

LOVE: THE PATHWAY TO *GOD*

JOURNEY BACK HOME

On our journey home to *God,* we become aware that sometimes we appear to walk backwards. Sometimes we may walk very far back, as far back as several lifetimes.

Other times we may walk back not so far but to our early childhood in this life time. Other times we may walk a short distance, a year, a month back. Sometimes we may get confused about the back and forth movements as they manifest in our dreams. Confusion may come because we know that when we set out on a journey to go to a specific place, we move forward, not backwards. If we spent time moving back and forward on the road we probably may never reach our destination in a timely manner. But the journey back to God is different. It's not a linear path.

Sometimes when we feel spiritually energized, we may find ourselves revisiting the distant past. Why? Because we have gained enough strength to move far to face and resolve an unfinished problem that impact us today.

We come to realize that going back to face our past and resolving them is an essential part of our growth process, and one way I know this can be facilitated is with the help of trained spiritual travelers. We make these visits in order to untie karmic knots that may be hampering our forward movement. The karmic knots create clouds that stand between us and divine love. The karmic baggage can weigh us down on our upward ascent home to God. Once knots are untied, resolved, let go, we are rendered lighter, with greater ease we can now soar more freely closer toward our divine home.

We can therefore take comfort in knowing that our trips backward into our past are indeed trips forward back home—home to God.

GOD SPEAKS TO US IN MANY WAYS

God has innumerable ways that It talks to us. Not only through the human voice, which is so commonplace that the message from God goes unnoticed many times. But there are other more profound ways not commonly known to most people. One way God communicates to us is through Sound. Sound manifests itself as sounds of nature as well as human language in the outer world we live in. Some Sounds are audible and others are inaudible. These outer Sounds are echoes of pure inner Sounds that issue directly from Godhead. Hearing the inner sounds at a deeper level can open one to the Divine

Spirit. This process of opening yields spiritual purification. It purifies, uplifts whoever has the good fortune, training, purity, and self-discipline to hear it. It is the music of God coming to bless you. Coming to uplift you and free you from conditions that are holding you down in the meshes of human consciousness.

It's a true blessing to hear the sounds of God in their many pristine forms.

Not many people have the ability to do so. It requires training at the feet of a spiritual master to open oneself to these inner sounds. Such techniques abound in the teachings of Eckankar, the path of Spiritual Freedom. For those who wish to hear these sounds, they can try out some of the spiritual exercises taught in Eckankar. They are not designed to change your spiritual belief, but if anything, they are designed to deepen your personal connection with Divine Spirit. They are universal and have a spiritually liberating effect on anyone who diligently practices them. To do them is a true privilege for they will transform you spiritually, making you a more spiritually awakened person than you were before. When you hear *God* speak through Its voice as Sound, you are blessed beyond words, beyond compare, beyond your wildest imagination.

Honor the Sound, appreciate the moment, fully embrace it with love and gratitude because it's God's presence you just experienced.

FOLLOWING THE
VOICE OF *GOD*

Whenever we set out to do anything of worth, we are never alone. There's always help by our side, but we are not often aware of it nor are we often willing to accept it. The reason is that we are, in truth, not aware enough thus not open to it. We seek it in more complex ways when in actual fact it could be simple and right in front of us. Because our expectations often run counter to new truth. We tend to look everywhere else save where it truly is, right before us, hidden within us, within our inner sanctum. The small voice of God comes through our inner chambers wherein answers to life lie locked away till our spiritual senses are sharpened enough to hear.

Sometimes the answers we seek are packaged as a puzzle. Sometimes the guidance may come as a direction to a more direct practical solution. Other times as a nudge to do something that will lead to a missing link, till eventually to our desired outcome. It seems that all the answers are set up so they can open our hearts to greater awareness of ourselves as divine beings. The process of gaining these answers become a learning tool about how spirit works in our life and the principles embedded in them. If we were to be given all answers on a silver platter, we would not learn about the laws of life therefore not grow spiritually. Without working for them, we would learn nothing spiritually. We would grow spiritually lazy, because we would have no exercise to strengthen our spiritual muscles. For instance, in the physical sense, we already know that the answer to gaining strength and building muscle is by physical exercise. This requires genuine commitment that we do it so many number of times regularly to build our muscles. We may know what to do but we may hate the process required to build the muscles needed to increase the strength to reach the desired goal. The same principle applies to building our spiritual muscles.

When we come to a point where we come to full practical realization, and look back, we'll find that we're no longer the same person who started off. By gaining the spiritual answers through listening to the inner guidance, we become spiritually transformed to a new being with expanded consciousness. We become a living and walking example of what it means to realize truth. Once we learn how to hear and follow the voice of God, we will begin to walk a direct path to God.

And no one can walk the path of truth for us, save ourselves.

THE KEY TO NONINTERFERENCE

Strive to live a clean life. A life can easily be tainted unknowingly by our encroachment on other people's lives either by purposeful intent or due to not understanding how our thoughts and actions interfere in other people's lives. Some meddling actions and thoughts may be born out of a mistaken belief that we need to render help to another when our help may not truly be needed. Such actions tend to serve only our egos. Listen to your heart to be guided so you can give help only where and when needed. If we render help when not needed, we maybe inadvertently be taking away their needed lesson or experience. This will do a disservice to that person. For a person may need to go through a situation in order for them to learn a much needed spiritual lesson in their life. With the lesson learned, one grows spiritually.

Other more subtle forms of actions that may cause us trouble is the act of trying to listen to God as we try to navigate through life can present a challenge if one expects to get the answer right away. Especially, when we have predetermined the answer and thus expect the same. This can lead to an interference in the listening process because we will be trying to manipulate the divine Spirit in trying to bend it to conform to our will to fulfill our desires. On face value, the intention may seem good, yet the process may be complex, at worst confusing and misleading as you unintentionally plunge into the psychic realm. How do you avoid this inadvertent slipping into costly Psychic realm?

The key lies in constant withdrawal inwardly from every situation to gain clearer insight into it. An urge to extricate an answer on our terms may engender an interference, an intrusion, in the process.

God operates in ways that are not always ours, so Its answers may come in Its own time and in its own way and not in our predetermined time and way. To avoid interference in any form, go with the flow, give up all to gain all. Let go of all to have all. Surrender all to embrace all. Stop needing all to be needed. Stop controlling all, to gain freedom and control over oneself. Stop needing anything material from within so only what you need gravitates toward you. Stop all forms of acts that lead you to meddle with anyone's life, so your life is not contaminated. With that, you will lead a clean life of noninterference.

GOING BEYOND

Our experiences are determined by our thought processes, our expectations, our beliefs, decisions we make, and our considerations both on the inner and outer. The outer manifestations of these things take longer because of matter, energy, space, and time (MEST) that hold sway over our life here. In the inner, our thoughts manifest more quickly because the MEST factor is much less. The higher we go within, meaning less MEST the quicker these thoughts manifest.

We are where we are because we've accepted this reality as is. To go beyond where we are now, we need to start letting go of our current thinking, acknowledging that our thinking and expectations are limited to what we see and believe. If we let go, let the Divine Spirit guide us to where it needs us, the hold we've imposed unknowingly on ourselves will be lessened or be removed. And the Divine Spirit will have the greatest influence and the power to take us beyond. Beyond into the inner unseen God worlds. Beyond this world of appearances exist a world that is real but operates at a higher level of vibrations, beyond the range of perception of human vision. To see beyond, one ought to employ spiritual senses that are adaptive to a higher unseen world. Getting a glimpse of the unseen world changes one's outlook at life. One begins to view life a little more clearly, understands a little better the relative reality we live in, fear of death goes away for one now knows that life continues beyond this world.

HELPING OTHERS

What does it entail to appropriately help others? At a personal level, stick with what is spiritually right without bending and reject what is spiritually wrong without compromise, but be smart, wise and considerate in your approach. By so doing you will win over *God*. You will create positive movement in the ethers. You will help move life forward not only for yourself but for others too - by efforts that are right and firm yet uplifting. You become an individual who others recognize and respect. Because through your actions of courage based in uncompromising truth, you touch other Souls at their core.

Giving yourself to life involves some measure of risk. Risk, because one may go against the status quo, thus rock other people's boats, stretch them beyond their comfort zone, thus throw them off. You may be going against the grain. So be wise about it and how you proceed. Being selective in who you give of yourself to without being taken advantage of. Being wise about whom to trust and render help where needed. Never render help out of mistaken sympathy in which you enable laziness.

Don't do for others what they can do for themselves when help is not needed. If you were to do so, you would be playing unintended retrogressive role in that person's life. Give of yourself only when there's a real need to uplift another, bring a measure of comfort, needed help, a shoulder to lean on and a change in society for the good of all.

LETTING GO SO GOD CAN TAKE OVER

What do you actually let go? And how do you do that and why? Often we tend to rigidly hold on to our plans that we resist any unexpected changes without realizing that sometimes these changes may be an intervention from God trying to show us a better way. To let God take over, start by letting God guide you in what you plan to do today and tomorrow. Resist the tendency to want to run things with only your self-will. When you rely on your own personal efforts, you restrict the spirit flow. You must let go of your plans for the day and leave them in the hands of God. In letting go, you are allowing the hand of God to have a role in your plans. It may change your plans, but rest assured it is always for the better.

So trust God, entrust it with your life and all will be well. It's Divine Spirit's nature to move things well in order; however, be reminded, it's not always our idea of order. So be patient when you surrender your life to the will of God. It may turn things upside down, yet truly it's turning things about because your way was wrong.

Our knee jerk reaction is often to resist this change because we lack the awareness and understanding that it is for our own good. We fight tooth and nail, refusing to go in the new direction because it may feel unfamiliar, uncomfortable and uncertain or maybe inconvenient. And it should because it's a new way, yet the right way. Such is a feeling one gets when you let go of your self-control over your life. Suddenly you get a call from unexpected person. It may be God's way of saying here is a new direction to take.

Or you may feel a nudge to call someone, act on it, because it may be God's way of telling you to take the next step. Just remember, don't wait around for God to come down and start doing things for you that *It* can only do through you.

Just let go, and be watchful for new directions, insights, new ideas, dreams, waking dreams, new opportunities, and golden-tongued wisdom.

Stay alert for God may speak anytime, to bring good news needed for your next step.

MOVING CLOSER TO GOD

Moving closer to God may start by one, firstly doing things that one understands are good, in other words, Godly. And it's this godliness in things you do that takes you to a level beyond where you are. You transcend where you are to get to the next higher place. A place of greater freedom and of greater space. This is how you walk and take steps toward God from whence we all came from. And that's your mission, to walk back to God. If you don't, you are either walking in the same spot or backwards. It is helpful to keep in mind that this is not a competition, move at your own pace, don't compare yourself to others, because you have no idea what their quest on their journey may be about.

Remember, God's plan for you is not to regress to immature state. Because God's not backward, IT is always moving things forward. Remember what lies in the now is what *God* is. Thus well-lived today in alignment with God's will as much as is practical will make tomorrow a better day. And it's forward where God wants you to go. So move on ahead.

Should you feel tired, rest if you must, and should you fall as it may happen innumerable times, by God, pick yourself up and trudge along. It's in getting back up that we awaken to greater realization, if only a moment, of our divinity and eternal nature.

We will eventually come to an awakening that we must trust and love God first in order to move closer to God.

LOYAL SERVANT

How do you become a loyal servant of God? Loving God should be your daily practical exercise. It is in doing so that you begin to allow God to work more actively through you.

Godlike qualities will begin to show in what you do. When you actively involve God this way, you will have began to unravel the secret of life, which involves making a manifestation of Godlike qualities that comes from spiritual upliftment. These Godlike qualities keep you centered, happy, organized, courageous, wise, patient, virtuous, kind, strong, above all, loving. Through sacrifice, you will come to a greater understanding of what loving God means in the real sense.

By giving of yourself to life where and when needed and where and when you are able, you will begin to tap into higher consciousness. The nature of this state is to serve life.

So if you love God above all else, you will want to serve life selflessly.

With that, you will become an integral part of life and become its loyal servant not in a slavish blind way, but truly in a very conscious, willing, and loving way.

THE PARADOX OF LOVING GOD

God, in the abstract sense, in its apparent invisible state to human eye, may not be easy to love, so we are left with loving its manifestations that are directly accessible and relatable to us. Since God is in spirit form or formless, it makes sense to forego use of our physical senses and use our spiritual senses to connect with it. It is through our spiritual sight that we are better able to see and love God to a profound degree with our entire being. The act of loving God to whatever extent of your capability engenders a spiritual change in one. Everything to support your spiritual journey will begin to gravitate toward you to help you in your quest for deeper understanding of life and God. It's this gravitation that creates power in you. Power does not mean dominance over another. But power to inspire and draw people to love.

Love is what creates this vortex of attraction toward you. When this happens, you become the center of activity. Some people will be drawn to you in a manner that they want to serve you or attack you. To serve you because they see God's essence alive in you. Others may want to attack you because they're stirred to go beyond where they're but they are resistant to it. Thus their own inner fight against change becomes a fight against themselves and you, the purveyor of love vibrations.

So an attempt to love God may come across as both positive and may seem negative. Negative in the sense that it is wrongly perceived so due to one's resistance to open one's heart to God—a false perception by the mind. Positive, because once you surrender to It, your heart opens and gets filled with God's love, rendering your life spiritually richer and a joy to live.

HOW TO LOVE GOD

Realizing God is the highest attainment in one's life. Because it awakens Soul to its true nature as a conscious child of God. And in loving God, our lives are enriched a hundredfold. So it is wise to learn how to love God. Part of loving God is remembering to do every act for the good of all. This way your deeds are rendered Selfless and love becomes unconditional. With that in mind and heart, give love to God without reservation. Because loving God is your answer to the call of Soul.

Loving God can be easy yet difficulty for those who are held in bondage to this material world. Difficult for those who consider intellectualism as superior to love. Difficult for those afflicted by their own poverty in materiality. Difficult for those who are dominated and owned by their riches. Yet the key to loving God lies in one's ability to recognize that in loving God your life becomes a joy it is meant to be. Loving God starts with loving people close to you. That is the starting point.

LISTENING TO THE VOICE OF GOD

The voice of God is the inner voice that guides us in the right way. Once the voice speaks, it is spiritual truth. Once you hear it, follow it with determination and steadfastness. It's a way of God. It's a journey beckoning you to follow God. It is not always easy to follow because it takes us where often the routinized mind can't go. To places not always familiar, but always right. Not always easy, but always right. Not always logical, but always right. Not always what you expect it to be, but always right. That's just the way of God. Not always our ways. It takes us to new places, often uncharted territories. That's why it's a path of the courageous who don't need to follow a beaten path but find their own path within, who stand most alone for they have learned to lean upon the God power for support and guidance.

KEY TO LIVING A FULL LIFE

Is there a greater Key to a full life than love? Nah! so love God, love life, love all for in doing so, you will discover the gems of truth that exist in each one of them. In discovering these gems of truth, you must give them back to the world in order to receive more. In giving back, you are allowing God, through Divine Spirit to reach others who otherwise would not have done so. In receiving Life's gifts, you are opening your consciousness, your capacity for love to grow. You only receive if you create adequate room in your consciousness to receive.

How open or receptive you are can make a difference in how much love is allowed in. Trust is the keyword that opens the door so love can enter. Trust that all will go well according to divine will. Trust that things will be taken care of while you do your part at the human level.

Keep in mind that loving God and letting it work through you is the key to living a full life.

GOD IN CHARGE

When God is in charge life gets turned around. Life becomes rearranged in a new and better order. Rearranged such that a higher order emerges. When this happens, learn to keep it going. Keep it going in a forward direction. It's an exciting ride. A wonderful ride. But you must be courageous to ride it. It's a ride of God. Hang on and keep up or you will be dragged along unwillingly causing you to endure unnecessary suffering.

Yes, it's a ride on the wave of love to God. So go ahead and enjoy it. Because much as it is not easy at times, it brings joy, wisdom, love, freedom as its rewards. Go ahead, let it take you as far as it can let you, until you scream and can't take any more of it. Scream for it to stop for a needed respite, if only for a moment.

When God is in charge, It knows when you need to rest. All you have to do is trust It, and let It guide you, It will take you at your pace though there maybe different approaches to getting one's own spiritual guidance to ensure progress is individualized to fit one's pace. One of the ways this can be facilitated is by working under the tutelage and guidance of a spiritual master empowered to serve on the inner God worlds, such as Harold Klemp, the Mahanta, the Living ECK Master found in ECKANKAR. But you must determine for yourself what route fits your spiritual quest.

With proper spiritual training, your life shall be ever more balanced and a joy to live.

SERVING GOD

What does it entail to serve God. Start by placing your attention on God. Learning to become a God-lover. When you become a God lover, you love God above everything else. This implies following the dictates of God as much as is practically possible. This way it's like God acting through you. You are God's child gradually becoming its conscious child.

To be a conscious child is your innate nature for you carry the genetic spiritual makeup of God. To live up to it, you must reawaken your consciousness of It. Once the spiritual genes within you are activated, they get suffused and infused with the God force. Hence to keep this God force active in you, it is crucial to keep up one's spiritual duties daily. You will be surprised at what will happen to you. You will not be the same again. You will see life differently. God will be within you and without you. And serving God will become organic, a natural part of your daily life.

GREATER LOVE FOR GOD

Love is the key to life. A life lived with love and guided by love is indeed a superior life. It's a life lived in goodness. A life filled with happiness. And by its nature it brings abundance, fulfillment, excitement, and dynamism. In a more profound sense, it is a life spent in the sacrifice of the lower self for the higher self. It is in this sacrifice that we awaken to our higher self—Soul self. Banishing the illusory and temporary nature of this material life in our consciousness. Ushering in a paradigm shift and life as we come to know it in a spiritual sense is multi-dimensional in a real sense and a higher one governed by higher laws. Higher because we come to embrace life with higher permanent values of spiritual nature. It's in this permanency that we walk with new confidence and trust in higher power. It is this higher power we come to lean upon. This new inner reliance yields greater confidence, more respect and more love for life.

And it's in loving life more that we develop greater love for God.

LOVE: THE PATHWAY TO GOD

EXPRESSION OF SOUL

Each one of us is Soul. As Soul, you are potentially a loving entity, a divine spark of God. Infused in you are innate faculties and the power to do the impossible. You as Soul are equipped to do what you do and experience life the way you do and have the capacity to go beyond your present limited state. It is Soul that enables you to like what you like modified through the filter of your mind and its passions. So to be what you are as an individual with your own uniqueness is part of the expression of Soul. It is Soul's nature to love the way you do with capacity and potential to love more. So is the power to learn deeper knowledge with your inner senses once awakened. With faculties of Soul, you can transcend the limits of human consciousness and tap into the God power. To know God the way you do in your own way at your own level of acceptance takes engagement of Soul senses. To have the power to know that there's life beyond death and it's endless, requires purity of your heart. We can know that love exists everywhere only if our hearts, eyes, and ears are open enough to feel, see, receive, give, and experience it. You soon find that true love leaves no room for fear. A new understanding dawns that in detachment, you are freed from the shackles of the lower material world. You have the power within you to be whatever you want to be. The greatest of all love is love for God. You come to a new understanding that all life matters because God created all with a higher purpose. In knowing this, you are able to love life and God profoundly with your heart.

WHAT YOU ARE IN TRUTH AND IN SPIRIT

When you realize God has become a part of you in truth and in spirit, you become a conscious part of God in truth and spirit. This interchange exists at a certain level of consciousness. It's a level of total equanimity.

It's a level of spiritual and emotional balance. It's a state of beingness. It's a state of nowness. It's a level of inner connectedness with the essence of God. It's a level of pure divine love. It's a level of awareness that makes you stay grounded spiritually and physically. It's a level that no one else would understand save only yourself and those who have attained it.

This is a state of all giving, all sacrifice for a higher spiritual cause, for the greater good. That's what being in truth and spirit means in a practical sense.

MAKING LIFE BETTER

Making life better implies having more love come into your life. When you have love, you have God in essence. When you have love, you have God in spirit. When you have love, God lives in your heart. When you have love, life presents new opportunities. When you have love, the opportunities multiply for more profound life experiences. When you have love, life presents itself in a new light. When you have love, God presents itself in a way that you become aware of its guiding presence. When you have love, God becomes the predominant influence in your day-to-day decision making. When God becomes the essence and the basis of your life, all actions serve to make life better.

Thus it behooves you to follow God with every fiber of your being. God will in turn embrace you, protect you, infuse you with its infinite wisdom, freedom, power, and love.

IN GOD'S HANDS

How can we place ourselves in God's hands so we can be lifted to higher consciousness? Love is the key, it implies that it is the only force that opens the doorway to higher consciousness. It is this higher consciousness we aspire to live in. To live in this higher consciousness as much as possible is to live in God to the degree that we accept it. So the extent to which we honestly aspire to live in God, to be a part of God's presence is the extent to which you will extend your love to others.

The act of putting love in all we do yields a secondary yet more important effect.

It steers us in the right direction in our journey home to God. Each action imbued and driven by love brings us closer to our true nature. Our true nature is a happy and loving Soul. In embracing our true nature, we are embracing God, in actuality the spirit of God. It is through this reciprocal action that our marriage with Divine Spirit becomes one with each other. Our thoughts, our actions, our feelings become those of Divine Spirit. Touched by it, guided by it, sustained by it, induced by it. So that where ever we tread, we are on holly grounds. We are in God's hands. We are with God, home here and now, even though we may not always be aware of it.

PUTTING LOVE INTO THINGS WE DO

When you do everything with love, it becomes your main driving force. Love begins to infuse all your actions. It begins to guide all your actions. It begins to show you how to love better. It begins to teach you how to love life. It becomes the teacher of all your lessons. It begins to open doors which were closed due to a lack of it. It begins to lift you, protect you and comfort you. It begins to surround you with gifts from unexpected places. It begins to give you courage in things you feared. It begins to act as your pillar to lean on and gives you security. It becomes your only source of direction inwardly and outwardly. It becomes the basis for your moral compass.

It helps you distinguish wrong from right. It enables you to see God in everything. It begins to inspire your life and sets you on a path in which you begin to grow at your own pace and in the right direction home to its source point—the Godhead.

GETTING HIGHER TO THE NEXT LEVEL

Whenever you do something with love, with interest, with an unusual ability that seem to work out with unusual ease despite the obstacles placed along the way, you are bringing out the God essence. The spirit of God which you are bringing is that which touches others in ways that are not commonly touched purely by ordinary activities. The spirit is what makes the difference between fulfilling your mission as God intends you and carrying out something the ego creates for you.

Give yourself to God and you will be surprised how opportunities come up that enable you to fulfill the dream God has for you. When a new opportunity arises, be available to take advantage of it. Be adventuresome enough to execute the action which only God can do through you. Use what you have to achieve what you need to get to the next level. The only way to go is up— up to the next rung up, inch by inch, by listening to the subtle divine messages leading you higher toward the Godhead.

GOD, THE CENTER
OF YOUR LIFE

When God is viewed as the center of one's life, one's life becomes centered in God. This means living life for God, in God, with God. Living life for God entails sacrifice for greater good. Living life in God means all actions are carried out in the name of God. Living life with God meaning God becomes your daily partner in all you do.

You don't ever do things alone but in concert with God via trust. As you trust God, IT becomes more available to you. Lack of trust creates a gulf between your outer human self and God. So it behooves us to design our life such that all things we do become geared toward serving God. How do you ensure this is so? By daily attention on God as much is practically possible. It is not easy to do when the pressures of our daily life take up most of our attention. One practical approach to do is to set aside time for your daily prayers, meditation, contemplation or whatever you do to reconnect with your inner spiritual side in the privacy of your own life. It is advisable that you do it on a regular basis in order to bring about desired results.

GOD IS IN YOU AS YOU ARE IN GOD

This is the riddle you must uncover. It is a riddle that has haunted man from time immemorial. It's a riddle which if once unraveled, you will never look at life the same way. But first uncover the secret behind all secrets. A secret which is not a secret is that the answer to the riddle of God exists inside your heart. If you learn to reach in and stay there, make your daily residence there, spend time there, you will find that the riddle of God is more real than you realize as it gradually makes itself known to you. It's authentic, it is the ultimate truth.

Without understanding it clearly, one gets trapped in the meshes of the negative power. You can gain a good understanding of it by your daily commune with God with an attitude of surrender, sincerity, and trust in the unseen power. By listening to Its voice, you will gain deeper insights into your life. Once the insights are gained, apply them in your daily life, crystallizing them into a practical reality. And when you are ready, you will come to an understanding, experientially, that God is in you as you are in God.

As we practice talking to God, It will talk back to us in our inner recesses of our hearts. And in that inner sanctum, the riddle of God will be revealed unto you when you are ready.

SPIRITUAL STATE

How do you stay spiritual? Staying spiritual means a state of conscious connection with spirit. In practical terms meaning acting always from the place of love - unconditional love. Unconditional love meaning love that gives and never demands anything in return. To be in that state, one must place attention on God. Do whatever works for you in the path you follow. For those who maybe looking to explore other ways, you can try singing the secret name of God called HU as taught in ECKANKAR, the path of spiritual freedom. To do so, one must listen for the inner voice of God and watch for the light of God. By so doing one creates a vortex of spiritual activity that will vibrate out, touching all things that are around and through you. This revitalized state, this spiritual state, allows you to view life with spiritual eyes for a clearer and deeper view.

This in turn enables you to perform acts of kindness, fairness, respect, and love.

So, to spiritualize yourself sing God's name, listen, and act from the most high ground within you.

Such is a way to live from the spiritual state within you. And from this vantage point, your life will become a joy to live

GOD'S LOVE

THE HEART CENTER

The heart center is a spiritual center wherein we commune with God and from which we receive and give out love to others. Hence how we love will determine the state of our heart center. It is only when we love that we truly have life of meaning. Without love, our sense of happiness is diminished. We feel ill at heart. We lose zest for life. We lose a certain amount of energy. We lose the bounce and spring to our walk. Thus without love, we have to make more considerable effort to do a job we previously did with less effort. Because our heart which is the source center of this energy has contracted, thereby giving out less energy. The heart center is the central supply source. So when it shuts down, all activities shut down for the day, it could be for a month, a year or a lifetime. We wonder why our lives go on a downward spiral. Why our life seem meaningless. Why we are down on our luck. Why *God* seem to have forsaken us, not knowing we are truly the ones who have forsaken *God*. Our circumstances are the product of the choices we make, what we do and say.

It will serve us well to remember that life is a reflection and product of our choices.

Right choices will keep our heart center open and our lives in order again.

ACCEPTING GIFTS
FROM DIVINE SPIRIT

When we are ready for a new experience, life presents it. It could be a gift from *God*. The question is, if we miss or pass up the gift, does the gift present itself again later? Often we may not recognize it the first time. We may not recognize because it may appear too good to be to be true, too good to believe our eyes. Why does it seem so? Because we feel we are not worthy of it. But if it were so, that we are not worthy of it, would it even come to us in the first place?. We think it is not ours because in some instances we may be afraid. So we hesitate, because we believe when the gift comes, it will be at a convenient time. But these gifts have a knack of catching us off guard, when we least expect them. So we go on thinking all the negative reasons why we should not accept the gift. Then after we walk away, when our perception is clearer, we wish we accepted it after all. We wish we had more courage, humility or open enough to have accepted the gift on its first presentation.

First and foremost, we must accept in our consciousness that we are worthy.

We must accept the gift in our hearts; then only will we embrace it fully and with love.

If not, fear will inject self doubt in us and influence us to keep the gift at bay from us.

To accept the gift fully, let's first accept it in our hearts.

TRUTH AND LOVE YIELD GREATER LOVE

This applies to one as an individual. Love will show us how to love if only we can be humble enough to listen to the voice of life. Our sincere desire for truth, to live by the code of truth will always lead one to truth, greater truth which in itself reveals the presence of greater love. Love and truth coexist to build on each other. So that when you love truth, this love becomes the key that opens the door to the discovery of higher spiritual truth which in turn yields greater love.

Truth is an underlying force, the language of God, lost in the midst of the outer illusion seen from human perspective. Love is the untainted presence of the essence of God hidden behind the veneer of the lower worlds filled with guile, pain, deceit, and entrapment. These two elements of love and truth abound in unalienable coexistence in the higher worlds beyond matter, space and time.

So listening to God becomes the beginning of the process of discovery of truth beyond what meets the human eye in places we didn't think it existed. So it is to our spiritual advantage to love God for doing so, will lead us to higher spiritual truth, thereby expanding our hearts to greater love.

GIFTS FROM *GOD*?

The gifts from God serve a dual purpose: One, to enrich our personal lives; Second, to enrich and uplift society. In other words, gifts from *God* are not selfish gifts, they are selfless and universal in nature because all things made out of *God's* material are selfless. By receiving these gifts and using them for what they are intended, we bring more light into our lives and in others' lives. Gifts come in different sizes, ways, and forms. And it should be so, for each will perform a different function and serve a different purpose. So our role as recipients of God's gifts is to pass them on with love to the world at large. People who do so are always rising to new and higher spiritual heights and above mass consciousness.

Gifts from *God* are designed to make this world a better place, more peaceful, and livable place as we continue our slow steady, albeit often arduous journey home to *God*. It is in passing along these gifts that our sojourn here is rendered happier, more forgiving and more fulfilling.

STEPS TO RECEIVING GIFTS FROM *GOD*

What happens when we forget gifts from *God*? Life has a way of reminding us.

One way could be through someone telling us how good we are at something. By so doing, Soul is reminded, it's jolted out of forgetfulness. Now it's up to us to answer the call of soul and rearrange our lives and make necessary steps to start moving toward the cultivation of that gift. Thus setting a plan becomes the first essential step, then identifying and setting measurable and achievable short term and long term goals.

One key factor is the timeline to meet these set goals. As you set out to achieve the goals, though you stay committed to them, make sure you remain flexible in your approach, making adjustments as new information and help comes up along the way. Be aware that smaller non-target gifts may come up, stay open to receiving them for such maybe the link leading to the ultimate goal. For these small gifts are often a foundation and serve as link points to prepare grounds for our long term goal. So, appreciate equally the small gifts, for latent in them are eternal blessings, lying in them are the makings of potentially the ultimate desired gift. Such maybe steps we need to take in order to climb, rise, to reclaim our grander gift from God.

A gift when accepted and passed on for universal good, is a gift that will keep on giving.

CREATING HALLOW GROUNDS UPON WHICH WE WALK

Fully participate in life and do the best you can. Do all for God and not for Self. Do what you have to do as humanly possible and leave the results into the hands of *God*. This allows you not to influence the results of your actions by interference with human condition thus imposing limitations. You do so by stopping to attach yourself to the anticipated outcome of your actions. Go with the flow. This allows God to step in and take over where limits of your effort end. Staying open to the changes as they come about.

It's one way you work with a plan that way you don't interfere with whatever the natural course of action the results may take. After all is said and done, let go of the results of your actions. Seek no recognition for the product of your labor. Seeking credit and recognition makes the ego grow big, thereby limiting the impact of God at what you do.

Your duty is to focus on doing your best at the moment. It is through such an attitude that you manifest the qualities of God thus serve God. Once you serve God today, through your loving actions, you will create better future conditions.

By serving God today, we create hallow grounds upon which we walk tomorrow.

Our tomorrow becomes nothing short of a blessed tomorrow.

LOVING WISELY

Give love to those who deserve to be given love because they can return it faithfully.

Give goodwill to those who cannot requite your love. In other words, love discriminately.

For those who give you love, give your all from your heart. Maximize your effort in loving them, for then you are loving God through them. For others who cannot return your love, give only goodwill. In other words do not expend energy more than is needed.

Learning how to love so the law of economy in what we do enters all aspects of our lives.

You love God by loving those near to you. How can you love God if you can't love people that are close to you? The truth is you can't. You must learn to love people around you first, people you rub shoulders with before you can begin to understand the concept of what loving

God is. By loving those who are close to you, your heart easily begins to open because there is less resistance and there is the element of implied trust. When your heart opens, then you can start making steps toward loving God. Because the prerequisite to loving God is an open heart. It's an open heart that has the capacity to discern and embrace God's love.

The Soul, which is made from the same cloth of God, has inherent faculties to love God in a natural way. By loving God with your heart, you acquire higher love, unconditional love. So the progression is from human love, you graduate to higher unconditional love. With this love, you can love those around you with warm love and those not close with goodwill, also known as detached love or charity. Such is what our limited human capacity can handle. It's this love so extended to others that we enrich others' lives as it in turn enriches ours too. So go out and give love wisely, accordingly and appropriately with proper discrimination, for that is the way of this world.

ESTABLISHING A BETTER RELATIONSHIP WITH LIFE AND GOD

What does it mean to establish a better relationship with life? What role does love play in this? Does God have a role in this process? Does how we see ourselves impact our relationship with life and God? If God loves you, it doesn't matter how you see yourself. Whether you think lowly or negatively of yourself, God still loves you the same. It does not love you more because you do more, or because you love yourself more. Or you pray more or you have more money, God loves all things based on one's spiritual needs and level of acceptance.

It is the law of economy in action where love is not wasted where not needed. It loves you enough to sustain you. To get more, you need to give more love. You as Soul exist because God wills it so in spite of yourself. You being Soul thus spirit in nature, yet taking on different outer characteristics, you don't still change your fundamental substance as an atom of love, a happy entity that has latent power to commune directly with God via the Divine Spirit. So that God is always available through such spiritual mechanism if one wishes to reestablish one's connection with It. But here in the dual worlds, Soul, the real you, not the ego self, takes on varied aspects, sometimes positive but often negative outer self often tainted by mind passions. Because it is the mind and its passions that hold sway over your life.

When they say God loves you, it's you as Soul this reference is made to irrespective of whether you are considered bad or good and irrespective of your religion. It's Soul that God is interested in and its survival, growth and maturity. It is God's child that It wishes to return to its home to reclaim its throne as a loving child of God.

Soul is the real innermost make up of you, is indestructible and has capacity to love because in essence it is made from the same loving cloth of God. It inhabits aspects of God it was made with. Realizing these God aspects leads to greater understanding and better relationship with life and God

And when its child awakens to its true heritage, God rejoices.

SPIRITUAL MASTERS AMONG US

In this world, exist spiritual masters, known and for most part unknown to man, sometimes known as angels whose role is to help Souls seeking direction in their lives, seekers of truth, needing help in some way, maybe lost along the way in this warring world and beyond. They seem to all work under the aegis of God. They don't impose their will on anyone. Their conduct is one of the highest order with ethics unmatched by any human standard.

One fact not commonly known is that even among angels are levels of consciousness and roles. To that end, some angels serve within a limited sphere of human activity, higher ones such as ECK masters serve life at a much higher level, which involves helping souls who are on their next step toward spiritual freedom in this lifetime. These spiritual masters dispense their unconditional love to all and under all conditions. While at the same time allowing individuals their free will to chart their own course in how they live their lives, exercise their free will in how they love and who they choose to love and what spiritual path they choose that fits their individual consciousness.

Love is the modus operandi they use to connect, lift, and help guide those on their own inner path to self-discovery and eventually God consciousness. So, loving another as God would, enables one to love from a highest place within oneself—the place of Soul.

By giving love from the position of Soul, you will learn to love the highest in friends, family, and those you meet irrespective of their religion. People in other paths have their own spiritual guides they look to for upliftment for there are many ways to connect with God that will fit individuals at different levels of consciousness all over the world. It would be absurd to think there can only be one way as God is not limited to one select group of people. In the human state, we tend to limit God to what group It favors or belongs to. The truth of the matter is that God created all living forms therefore It belongs to all. So within this vast limitless realm of God, each person has the free will to choose a path that best fits that individual. The connection people establish with God is a personal one, therefore the journey to God is always personal even if people belong to the same church or religion as a group. So it is incumbent upon each person to determine for themselves what path fits them, what resonates with them. Forcing another into your religion is a violation of that person's right and freedom of choice of religion or path. Unless you know a person's spiritual needs, able to walk in their shoes, you are not in a position to choose what's best for them spiritually.

LOVING GOD KNOWING THAT YOUR WHOLE LIFE DEPENDS ON IT

Love God as if your whole life becomes nonexistent without IT. Love God as if you can't breathe without it. Love God as though this is the way life should be lived for your survival. Love God with everything you have got.

Love God without reservation. Love God to a point of intoxication. Love God to a point where you feel you cannot do without *It*. Love God because *It* gives you life.

Love God because *It* sustains you. Love God because *It* gives you all you spiritually and materially need. Love God because *It* gives you all you need for the trip back to *It*.

That means all life, even the minute detail of what might seem insignificant.

Because all is integrated and leads us back to the life source. That is *God* Itself.

LOVE: THE MOST IMPORTANT ELEMENT IN YOUR LIFE

It's love that elevates you from one level to the next. It's love that opens your heart to the gifts of God. It's love that makes you realize that you count and so does your fellow human being. When you have love, you have everything. Without love, you are lost in the entanglements of this material world. So lift yourself out of the morass of the lower world. Recognize the power of love. Let your heart be filled with love so that while you are on earth, your heart is ever in the heavens. Because after all your home is not here on earth, Soul which you are doesn't belong here but the God worlds. And it is through love that you can reclaim and reestablish your home in the God worlds.

YOUR TRUE DIVINE RESIDENCE

Love is the most important thing in your life because it is what makes your heart open up to God. In other words, it is the key to God. Therefore, you are able to enter God's house via love. Love is indeed your personal pathway to God. Try to work on expanding your capacity for love for it will lead you to God. In God you will find your true divine residence. Let it be your home where you dwell every day, every minute. Because that's where you belong as a realized Divine Spark of God. That's your real home as Soul.

While in the gym working out, new insights filled my consciousness:
Do every thing for God.
When you jog on the treadmill, do it for God.
When you work, do it for God.
Whatever you do, do it for God.
When you eat, do it for God.
When you walk, do it for God.
Let God be in every fiber of your being and actions.

LOVE IN EVERY ACTION

Love is an important aspect of our life. From a practical standpoint, simply do what you can to infuse love in what you find natural to do on a daily basis. It maybe one act or two or three, in which you are conscious of injecting love. Bear in mind that some days it will be easier to do and other times it might be difficulty to infuse love in your action. Do what works for you. Don't give up, Over time you will realize that you must have love as the only thing that matters in every action. This is what needs to be realized. This is what needs to be *acted* upon. This is important because this is what is going to make you a loving person. Without that you are just an individual like anyone else, in the fold of mass consciousness that does not understand the realities of higher love: That it must be manifested and not just talked about.

The nature of action will determine whether it's love or not. Once the action is love driven, it will benefit you and the recipient a great deal. But when it is not love driven, but power dominated, it benefits no one in the true spiritual sense in the long run. It may appear to benefit someone in the short run, but that is illusory.

It has no real power upon which to build on life, but instead takes away from life.

So, let love be infused in all your actions for that is the way of God.

THE INFLUENCE OF GOD

Without God in your life, you can't act or do anything of spiritual worth. Only engagement of God in whatever way you believe or view it, can make one's life meaningful and worth living. That means God being actively involved as the driving force in your actions. Since God uses love as the vehicle to build life, your life will expand to the extent that you allow love in what you do.

When God works actively with you, It will guide you to its Home. It will open your eyes to It's actions. It will free you from the shackles of this world. And once freed, you will soar freely to higher spiritual heights. In fine, you must love in order to have your spiritual life fulfilled. Fulfilled in the spiritual sense, yet all aspects of your life will also get enriched in the process. And that is the far reaching influence of God once allowed to be an active part of your daily life.

To sustain this positive influence, learn to do Godly things. Godly things are those things driven, sustained and expressed with love. Allow God in your life, not as an idea of it, but an active part of your daily living. This way you can maximize enjoyment of its greatest influence in your life.

LOVE AND ITS WAYS

Love as a force is not easily understood. Many times it is misconstrued to mean an emotional force. But yet in its true nature, it's above that. It transcends thought too. Since it goes beyond thought and emotion, it supersedes them in power. Such that living a life guided by love and infused with love allows one's thoughts and emotions to be refined. With love as a guiding force behind your thoughts and emotions, your ensuing actions will reflect high ethics. A life of high ethical standards is a life lived with love, fairness, understanding, consideration, and respect for Self and others. It is a life lived in harmony with Divine Spirit.

With love, one can't help but live one's life in an uplifting manner.

BECOMING SPIRITUALLY ALIVE

How do you become spiritually alive? You can start off by learning how to love God and keeping your heart open to God's love.

That way God fills you with love. The opening of the heart involves letting go of your hold on things, to allow new things to come in while actively participating in life. You must participate in life to be able to bring about life changes through love. To keep love flowing, you must give without asking or expecting anything in return.

Receiving is what follows after you have given. This happens because every action must have a counter flow of love energy for balance to be maintained. These actions must be done with love, with intention to build, to make life better, to advance society, to create conditions to facilitate learning about how to love God more. Each religion or path has its own way of praying to God or higher power or whatever name you call it, generally through daily prayers, meditation, contemplation or whatever method you use, but you must be able to integrate what you gained into your daily life for it to be of any value.

It's through your integration of love with your daily activities that you become spiritually alive. It's when you are spiritually charged with love and serve life by doing what you love to do that you can naturally and easily love God more.

MAKING GOD A DAILY REALITY

You can start to make God a daily reality by loving yourself as a first step. Loving yourself in a manner that it allows you to love others as you love yourself and as you would like them love you. In light of that, loving others, implies loving yourself. You cannot give love which you in the first place have not realized in yourself. Since we are made from the materials of God thus carry same characteristics of the essence of God, loving allows us to manifest these God qualities in a practical way. Loving of Self, Soul self at a much deeper level opens the way to loving God. In actuality, the spirit of God. Because it is through Divine Spirit that we come to know and love God.

And it is through Divine Spirit that we get to manifest Godlike qualities.

So remember that to love others, to love yourself, to love Divine Spirit is in and of itself loving God. And this must be done on a daily basis, making it an integral and active part of your consciousness. As we do so, we are making God a daily reality in our lives.

LOVING GOD

To love yourself is the first step in recognizing God's love for you. If you don't love yourself, it is difficult to love God. If you hate yourself, it is difficult to love anything outside of yourself. You can only give out what you have within you. If you have hatred, that's what you will give out consciously or unconsciously. Love changes everything.

Recognition of love is the dawning of the realization of the God essence in yourself and others.

God loves you whether you regard yourself a sinner, a bad person, unworthy, unlovable, hateful or a criminal. God still loves you. Because that's the nature of God. God loves all—period! God created all out of love, thus sustains all through love.

Therefore turning to God is in itself loving God.

And it is only through opening our spiritual eyes and ears will we be aware, in a more profound spiritual sense, what loving God truly means.

LOVE IN ITS TRUE ESSENCE

Love can constitute touching God with our heart in a way that transcends the mind.

Reaching out to God in a way that no human will can accomplish. Reaching into the heart of God in a way that only the heart can fathom. Being a part of that God essence in a way that thought is no longer needed to link oneself to God. Being a part of God consciousness in a way that love becomes an integral part of your being, a center of your existence from which all thoughts and actions spring.

Coming to the realization that God is love, love is God. The godliness you become a part of is the measure of the love you are able to give out to the world through selfless acts. Love itself is God in action. For all things done out of love, with love, for love are godly in nature even though their appearance maybe deceptively mundane.

So to understand love and express it in its true essence, one must awaken one's inner consciousness and learn to embrace God within.

GOD LOVES ALL

When God enters your life at a deeper level, it affects how you love others. The greater this depth is, the greater your love for others. So, allowing God to enter your life in a committed way without dictating to IT, expands your heart's capacity for Divine Love, and ability to pass it on to the universe where it truly belongs.

Open your heart and let love in, it's not intended for you to hoard it and hide it in your heart, but to pass it on to those who need it. To do so, you must let love guide you as to who merits it and in what way to share it. So that whatever you do, whatever you think, whatever you plan at its core there is love as a guiding principle.

You learn to do all for love alone. And with love, you attract more love, you partake of more love. So let God's love in. This essence of God will enter your heart, purify it, and with the power of love reach all within your orbit of experience and grace them with its loving presence.

On account of that, you will become a joy to those who know you as you will leave them a little happier, a little better, and a little more loved than before.

LOVE IS GOD

It is true about pure unconditional love being of God. It's the one truth that's absolute.

Because without love, there is no God and without God there's no love. The two are inseparable. God is the ultimate primary source of love. Pure unselfish love at whatever level is an expression of God. And everyone has a chance to express God in their own way that fits them.

Without love, you cannot move forward in your spiritual journey. Without love, you cannot build on anything with any measure of meaning and longevity, spiritually. It's only God's love that builds and sustains life even though people are not always aware of that. Without an element of love for anything, nothing lasts for long. Because God builds and sustains through love. It's the only stuff that assures an upward ascent to higher, glorious spiritual heights.

So to love God is to build life. So always strive to do things that are positive, truthful, and uplifting and life will repay you well.

Learn to love God because with that your life will change for the better. A life guided by God's love, filled with love, founded on love is indeed a blessed life.

GOD LOVES YOU BECAUSE IT LOVES YOU

God loves everyone of its creation because IT created all living forms through love.

So if God loves you, it doesn't matter whether you love yourself or not; how you see yourself is immaterial. Whether you think lowly of yourself, God still loves you the same. It does not love you more because you do more or love yourself more. God loves, because it loves, because it's its nature to love. It's God's law that It loves all regardless. But how much of God's love you receive is up to you. It is predicated on how much capacity you have to give and receive love.

You being Soul, though you take on different outer characteristics, your basic nature remains the same and all it needs is love for its sustenance. And that's where God's love comes in. God sustains Soul through love. You as soul, not to confuse yourself with ego self, take on different outer aspects; some positive and others negative for the express purpose of learning about itself and life. So when it's said God loves you for what you are, it's you as Soul above and beyond the superficial aspects that God is most interested in.

What you are includes aspects of your individual way of expressing God's love through your actions, your innate abilities, gifts, skills, and many other ways through which Soul expresses itself through love in this world. Engaging In such is the beginning of Self recognition of what you are as Soul: The innermost loving part of ourselves God loves and is concerned with.

Your participation in what you love becomes a window through which God makes its presence known in your life.

GOD LOVES YOU NOW, EVERY DAY, AND FOREVER

God gives love to all, but does IT give more to those who need it more.? The more you need by virtue of giving it out, the more you receive by virtue of creating more room to replenish it. When you hoard love, it fills up your cup, the surplus overflows, your life spirals out of control, out of balance, because you close the channel on the outgoing end. To regain balance between the inflow of love from God and outflow at the outgoing end, you need to pass the love to others, to life, to the universal where it belongs—to serve a purpose. Keep in mind that *love* is purposeful.

Once love is passed on to where it's needed, it will fulfill a higher purpose. It's this proper giving of love that one finds a balance. Proper discrimination is called for to determine where, when, to who it must be given. So who ever the recipient is, benefits from it. This should be an ongoing process which requires one to keep the heart open.

And how you conduct yourself will bespeak of your relationship with life. Love is what determines the quality of your relationship with life.

The continual flow of love keeps your heart open to the love of God. With this conscious loving, continually, you will realize that God loves you now, everyday, and forever.

THE NATURE OF SOUL

Because you are Soul, God loves you for who you are as Soul. Soul is the element of God that contains the qualities of God in action. God in action is the Divine Spirit. Remember that what you are as a loving Soul is what you must recognize, express and be while here on earth.

Many a time we act, behave, do things as though we were not Soul, a spark of God.

For the most part, our behavior is not reflective of what we are as loving Souls. The daily pressures of our daily lives make us lose and forget our true identity as Soul. To regain our spiritual footing, we need to slow down a little, contemplate upon the permanency of our identity as Soul. Once we begin to delve within ourselves, in the quietude of the moment, we will gradually start to awaken to our greater Soul self.

We must resist engaging in negative elements that taint Soul and work to consistently be ethical in order to remain in that Soul state. It's a state of love, balance, happiness, moderation, patience, wisdom, freedom, love and strength.

It is in staying in the positive state that we reclaim what we are as loving Souls.

For that is the true nature of Soul and is what God loves us for what we are as Souls.

GOD EXISTS IN ALL THINGS

When you believe God exists in all things, you are likely to embrace life more fully.

When you realize love is an aspect of all existing things, your attitude toward life changes. With this new attitude, you will begin to recognize that every experience has a spiritual aspect to it. Your respect for life heightens. You gain insight and recognize that all life experiences happen for your benefit, therefore designed to serve you and to move you closer to God. Life is no longer what you've always viewed it to be, that there is more to it than that viewed with the outer eye. You discover that life is now an integrated manifestation of the play of God.

To love life with such an attitude is to embrace life without fear, for one knows God exists in all things. This awareness itself should instill higher love toward life. And your relationship with life becomes that of respect and love for all life in whatever form. Thus partaking in life in the right way is equivalent to participating in God's daily presence. Because God is everywhere and in everything around us.

GOD'S WAY

God loves you. It created you and inserted a seed of love into your heart. God loves you even when you don't realize It does. When you love God, life changes around you, a new direction is paved, new help comes along—sometimes unsolicited, protection comes when needed, love comes from unexpected places, all designed to help you on your journey home to God.

So be well advised to follow God's way because God's way is always the right way.

Man's way dominated and controlled by the ego leads one astray. God's way is always right and leads one in the right direction. God's way is a highway, a clear way, though for most part travelled via byways and can at times be rugged. The caveat is that it is only clear to those whose spiritual eyes are open. It can be a rugged path in some respects. Ruggedness intended to temper you, to make you stronger, wiser, and more loving. So you can climb the ladder of God, rung by rung, a little easier as you apply special effort to travel along your own path within and without.

This is the way God is, this is the way God guides and takes you home. God will always bring you home in a way that fits your pace in Its own way. However these may at times seem different from your ways. Adjust your path to God's way, for it is a highway to the heavens that few tread. It's God loving you as a unique individual and it's here to reclaim you as Its child if you let It. When you are ready for your next step in your quest for spiritual truth, a spiritual master will appear or another path or religion will come before you or you may be drawn to it.

THE MISSING LINK

God loves you in ways you will never fully understand. God remains linked to you through love. Love is a line of communication that God uses to keep in touch with you. Love is the way God serves and sustains all *Its* creation. Love is what keeps you nourished spiritually. Love therefore is Soul food that Soul cannot do without.

Love awakens and opens one's heart to that inner link with God. Love is the only way God holds the entire world together. With love, you know you are with God and God is with you.

With love, you are in the zone that puts you at one-ment with God. With love, the missing link with God gets re-established.

BE LOVING! BE GIVING! BE WISE!

The love of God permeates all strata of one's life. There are no obstacles it cannot overcome. There are no mountains it cannot climb. There are no issues it cannot tackle.

There is nothing that can obscure it where it's needed to make its presence known. Love will continue to come to you whether you accept it or not if and when there's a spiritual imperative for its action. That's God doing its will. Generally, it will pour in amounts you allow to flow through the door you've opened for its passage. The wider you open the door, the more of God's love you receive. The more you receive, the more space you will need to create for its storage. Yet the paradox is you cannot fully store it. You need to pass it on or you will suffer the ill effects of an overflow. An excess of it will dissipate and accomplish nothing.

Learn to channel your love to accomplish more productive service in whatever form possible. Be active, be loving, be giving, be wise, and simply love; but give your love wisely, selectively where and when needed in this world.

RECOGNIZING GOD'S LOVE ALL AROUND US

Love for God opens our hearts to more love. Love for God means more than just words. It means love for God's creations—all living things, within the limits of your capacity. And those you can't love, you give them your good will.

When you love a dog, it's a creation of God you are loving—the Soul of a dog. The outer aspect is the manifestation of God as its byproduct—an aspect of an extension of the inhabitant—Soul. This love is that which transcends the outer appearance. Love is that which connects Soul to Soul in a way that eludes human understanding. It is that which honors the divinity of another Soul.

Soul is often overlooked because it lies hidden behind covers of its physical embodiment. Thus it behooves us to love the manifestations of God in whatever form they appear. And if we don't like the form, we should at least go past that form, to Soul.

By so doing, it gets easier to love another as Soul despite the physical barriers. We should awaken to the fact that all things around us have God essence in them despite their outer imperfections. Besides, nothing is perfect in this world.

In looking beyond the physical imperfections, we'll recognize God's love all around us. We will then live our lives recognizing that it's God that gives us love through the gift of life all around us.

OPEN YOUR HEART TO RECEIVE GOD'S LOVE

When God gives you love, It Knows what you need and how you can receive it. God gives only in proportion to what you can receive and handle. God gives only when you are ready in your consciousness. When you are too expectant, you may not receive because you may be too tensed. When you are relaxed and not expecting anything, you may receive the gift because it's in the relaxed state that we stay open to receiving. Inner tension causes closure of inner doors and this cuts off the flow of Divine Spirit thus we lose connection with God.

So relax, let the Divine Spirit flow, keep your heart open in readiness to receive the gift of love. Love is the only key that can open your heart. An open heart is needed in order for you to receive love and be able to pass it to the universe. Whereas when you are tense, keeping everything to yourself out of fear, you inadvertently leave no room for love. When relaxed, your heart opens and gets into the receptive mode, letting go of fear while letting love in.

So open your heart, keep it open for God's gift of love to be received in greater measure.

GOD LOVES YOU

God loves you for what you are. You are what you are because God loves you.

God loves because God loves all Its creations. God created all things out of love as the ground substance. Love is the building material God uses to create Life. Things: meaning animated and apparent inanimate objects. All that exists has a source either directly or indirectly from God. God created you with love and because you are in essence love substance as Soul.

Being love by nature, you ought to act so as to reveal your true inner primary divine quality—love. Love should be the mainstay of your actions. Love should be the prime mover in all you do, all you think, and all you feel. God loves, thus it behooves you to be humble enough, patient enough and spiritually awake enough to recognize and appreciate God's love in whatever form it comes to you. Open your spiritual eyes and ears so as to recognize your divine place in its all encompassing, all loving, all forgiving, all inclusive limitless consciousness.

GOD LOVES EVERYONE

God loves everyone because *It* created them all in *Its* image. God creates because *It* loves. God loves because that's how *It* functions. God therefore is the Master of love for all Its creations.

We are to love God, our creator for what It is. By loving Its creations we are loving aspects of God manifested in different forms—human and animal kingdom alike. In the human state our capacity for love is limited, from a practical stand point. We need to recognize that it is the inner spiritual makeup that we get to love, transcending the outer conditions, getting straight to the inner being. This results in unconditional love, the higher form of love we ought to strive to give. To sustain it, we need to place less emphasis on the outer, yet not wholly disregard the outer part of ourselves, for it is a temple of our inner being—Soul. Looking at the higher self—Soul self, as we do so, our connection with others gets deeper. We then can love others without conditions and without being judgmental.

As a first step, we first learn to love ourselves. By so doing, we are better able to extend our love to those we choose to be close to and goodwill to all others.

LOVE AND GOD ARE ONE

Remember when you love God, you are in actuality loving life. Loving God and loving life go hand in hand. You cannot love one without the other. Loving life is a form of loving God. That which makes you love is the essence of God. Which means the more you love, the more you partake of God's richness. The more you give of yourself with love, the more you enhance your relationship with God. Thus it behooves us to love life, embrace life, love others.

It is only by loving others, being open to life and new experiences that we grow in our capacity for more love. Love God through loving life for love is the common denominator in all living things. In loving life and God's creations honestly, you will realize that love and God are one.

THE FORCE OF LIFE

Love is the force of life that drives life forward. Love is the force that makes life a treasure that it should be. Love is the force that expands life. Being a life force, it takes action to make it a reality. It takes a heart that is pure to manifest it fully. It takes an open heart to embrace it. It takes purity of feeling and awareness to appreciate its depth. It takes candor and grit to fully give it uninterruptedly. It takes patience to learn life's hidden lessons well. And once we catch this wave, this energy, this principle, our life changes. Only then do we verily live a life to the fullest. A life filled with adventure balanced by joy. A life whereby we meet life's challenges with love and creativity instead of solely the force of self will. It's a life lived with love. A life filled with changes and hurdles that serve to propel us higher and higher to new heights.

The higher we go, the more of a life force we give. And the more we receive.

In giving and receiving we become balanced in the outflow and inflow of the life force called love. And such is the intensely profound power of this life force.

THE FORCE OF LOVE

Love is the force that builds, holds life together and makes life possible. It takes work and right effort to express it. It takes purity of heart and honesty to manifest it.

It takes commitment and a selfless heart to embrace it. It takes purity of emotion, thought and feeling to appreciate its value. It takes courage to give it under all circumstances.

It takes patience to learn its many varied subtle ways. Once we catch this force, apply it properly, our lives become ever more fulfilled. A life enriched with unparalleled courage, joy, love, and wisdom. Yet it is a life not devoid of challenges. Except this time, the challenges are met with a loving heart, without fear. A life lived without fear is indeed a blessed one. It's such a life that the challenges are met with flexibility with an understanding that they are there to help us move along on our journey home to God.

And the higher we go, the further we can see into our future. And the more we gain deeper insight into our life. And the better we can serve others and all life with love.

As we serve life with divine love, we become a living, walking, expanding magnet of love.

Such is the nature of the force of love.

LOVE, THE ESSENCE
OF ALL LIFE

How do you hear the voice of love? Go within to hear the voice of love. It is by going within that we begin to understand love in its pure form. It is by going to our inner consciousness, to that state of our highest viewpoint that we access this deep love. Let us go within to know that love sustains all life. It touches all aspects of life. Love reigns supreme in all animated forms because love is life itself.

To have love in one's life at a conscious level on a daily basis is to live a life of love, governed by love, sustained by love, blessed by the magic power of love. Look to your heart to understand the true language of love. Its language is truth. Its language aims at awakening you to its ways that are so many, so subtle, yet so common place that often we overlook them.

Listen to the voice of love in all things that come into your life. Since all life has in it at its epicenter the essence of love, you will see it if you keep your heart open. For only love in your heart can see love in other things. And the degree to which you realize love in yourself is the same degree to which you will recognize it in others. So open your heart and you will begin to see love in all things. You will come to a point where you recognize that nothing has life unless love is breathed into it. Nothing exists unless love is at its center of its existence for it is love that renders it alive. Take out love and the physical shell ceases to have life. So look to love for a life of greater love. Look to love for a happy life. With love, your life has meaning and purpose.

With love you have a reason for your existence. We exist to discover the power of love. If we can travel this path that can lead us to the discovery of more love in its pure and higher form, our lives will likewise be elevated in proportion to how much of love we are able to embrace and give out. For it is in accepting this love that we undergo a transformation. It is in giving it back to life that we grow in our capacity for more love.

So learn to receive, embrace, and share this wonderful blessing. Remember that it comes into your life to bless you, to lift you, to make you a better vehicle for God's love to those you serve. You will become an ever expanding channel for the greater good. So rejoice in its presence in your life. Keep your eyes and ears open so you can see it when it comes. It may come in a form of a person, a pet, a hobby, a job, a talent or a simple gift and any number of ways. It may come daily and daily you must pass it on and share it in some way. Never miss an opportunity to give it where and when needed. Soon you will become a magnet of love. You will draw people to you for love has magnetic properties, building properties, sustaining properties, because it is the essence of all life.

ANOTHER STEP HIGHER

We are all on our journey home to God whether you know it or not. We each have to determine for ourselves which direction to take spiritually. If you are satisfied with where you are spiritually with your current religion or spiritual path, then that is exactly where you belong, stay there, no need to look further. But if you are not satisfied, and you are not getting spiritual answers you need from it, then you may want to continue searching till you find the path that fits your spiritual quest for there are many out there. Whether you agree or not, at the end of the day, we all want to move another step higher in our quest for spiritual truth.

There are many religions or spiritual paths designed to lead their respective followers to God and they are all valid to the extent that they may provide their followers the answers they may need at their stage on their spiritual journey. All these established religions have a common thread of truth running through them. So that whatever religion fits you, there is truth in it that you may need for your spiritual succor. But if you feel you have outgrown a path, as it may happen in some instances, and you are no longer getting the answers you need, then it is wise to move on and search on till you find one that fits your spiritual quest. There are many to choose from, to name but a few, Christianity, Buddhism, Islam, Hinduism, and even less known spiritual path called ECKANKAR, the path of Spiritual Freedom, at its helm is its spiritual leader Sri Harold Klemp, The Mahanta, the Living ECK Master who operates both outwardly and inwardly to help his students establish a personal connection with Divine Spirit. He is not worshiped and under his tutelage, protection, and guidance helps them toward attainment of spiritual freedom in this lifetime.

Since God is eternal, and life is ever evolving, as it issues from the eternity of God, our quest for spiritual truth is endless.

ABOUT THE AUTHOR

 Eric Chifunda is a naturalized American citizen. He was born in Zambia. He resides in New York City. He is an occupational therapist who works as an independent contractor. He is also an artist who intertwines abstract, representational and visionary forms in his artwork. He strives to create art that is uplifting.

He is also an actor known for independent films such as *Slave Warrior* (nominated as a finalist at Hollywood Black Film Festival, San Francisco International Film Festival, and Atlanta Black Film Festival in 2007) *Return of Spade*, *This America* and its sequel *On the Run Again*, and *Cultures*, a pilot TV comedy series, written and directed by Oliver Mbamara.

This is a spiritual self-help book with wisdom on how to live an uplifting life with love as a guiding principle in all one does. Learn about different ways love manifests itself in everyday life, its ways, its impact, its reality, and how deeper understanding of it can enrich your life and others, and bring about life fulfillment. Since we all have a spiritual side, irrespective of one's religion or spiritual belief, we in some way, carry within us the message of love from God to be shared with others. To that end, the message of love can come from anywhere; animals, a child, a stranger, a beggar in the street, a friend, a rich person, a poor person, a co-worker--practically from anyone irrespective of one's religion or socioeconomic standing in life.

Hopefully, as you read this book, in it you find pearls of wisdom and the message of love to lift your spirits, inspire you to live a life of more love, more joy, more freedom, and an expanded understanding of life beyond its outer superficiality.

To view some of his Artwork please go to www.artworkbyeric.com

CPSIA information can be obtained
at www.ICGtesting.com
Printed in the USA
LVHW031559100221
678949LV00002B/337

9 781633 383227